I0729295

Tin's Tale

And Other Stories of Fraun

Tabatha Shipley

Tabatha Shipley

Dear Reader,

The book you are holding in your hand is a set of six short stories that take place in the Kingdom of Fraun. It is intended to either introduce you to or accompany the full Kingdom of Fraun series. It will answer a lot of questions about certain character's backstories. Enjoy.

Kingdom of Fraun Books

Breaking Eselda

Redeeming Jordyn

Training Tutor

Empowering Sawchett

Also by Tabatha Shipley

30 Days Without Wings

Projection

A Spark of Magic

Noises From the Other Side

Table of Contents

Secrets in Enchenda

My name is Selena. I am Queen of Enchenda and I am penning this scroll under extreme distress. It is my hope that as Queen of Enchenda, I will be able to right the wrongs I am about to put in this scroll. Doing so may well be the fight of my life. The council doesn't want these things coming out. The council doesn't want me to speak of them. I will do my best to keep this history from being erased, but I may not succeed. If you find this scroll, share it wide. Keep my family legacy alive.

To help you understand my turmoil, I need to explain a little history of my realm. Enchenda was the oldest son of Oberian the Second, we know this. He was born to Suzeth, the wife who gave him only one son. In other realms, it is whispered that we were the disappointing legacy right from that moment. When all other wives were able to give Oberian the second multiple children, Suzeth bore only Enchenda.

Enchenda took a single wife, Antwanet. They bore two children, Charles and Salen. Charles was older and would therefore be considered the heir of Enchenda. He would lead humbly and be trained in the ways of our realm. He married Elena. Elena bore two children, both girls. Selena and Suzette. I am Selena, the eldest daughter, and rightful heir following my father's rule as King of Enchenda.

But the reason I write this scroll is that nothing is ever as simple as it seems in the Kingdom of Fraun. The wall in my family home could easily relay this history to you as I have written it here. The real history is being erased and it needs to be told wherever we can spread it.

Suzette is younger than I am by only four annuals. She is bright, friendly, and beautiful. Around the realm, she has always been more popular than I am, although I was always slated to be Queen. King Charles, my father, lives in the royal home in town. As is expected, my mother, Suzette, and I live there as well. This is all as you would expect.

Since she is not needed to rule, my aunt Salen lives in a common household with her husband, Mark, and their daughter, Eseldena. Eseldena is very young, barely able to speak. My mother would not approve of me having this information. In her mind, Salen's family is dead to us. Enchenda needs my father to rule as their king. Then, when he passes, Enchenda will need me to rule as their queen. My mother desires for me to marry and bear children so that Salen's children and her line are never needed to rule our realm.

My mother is not of royal blood. She was born to a common family in Enchenda and promised to my father at a young age. Neither of them has ever been courted by another. They have both worked hard to make sure Enchenda is respected. They want our realm to be the respectable realm that my grandfather, from whom we are named, intended it to be. We cannot disgrace the family name. In my mother's opinion, needing my Aunt Saren to rule because our line was unable to bear out would be disgraceful.

But this is not the reason I write this scroll. My mother's high expectations are to be expected and, certainly, nothing I cannot handle. No, I pen this scroll because my sister Suzette broke those expectations in the worst possible way and it has led to something unimaginable.

As a young royal, my sister began sleeping with a common citizen of Enchenda without first conceding to marrying that citizen. She confided in me that it was happening. I encouraged her to approach our parents and tell them of the affair. I told her to request to be married.

Likely, they would allow this marriage. Assuming I can find a suitor appropriate to hold the title King of Enchenda by my side, my sister would not be needed to rule. Who she married would not be Enchenda's problem. My mother would view this in the same way she views my Aunt Saren, I was sure of it.

She took my advice. I am ashamed to admit now that I was wrong. My parents disagreed with the match. In a huge row, they forbade Suzette to marry this man. They argued that, although he is a decent enough man by Enchenda's standards, he is not worthy of the royal family home. Suzette tried to argue that they could find housing elsewhere in town, as Aunt Saren had done. This, they argued, would be beneath us. The answer, according to my parents, was simply that Suzette "do better for Enchenda" although it was unclear what that meant. They were unaware at the time that she was already sleeping in his bed. I neglected to tell them.

Three fortnights later I learned Suzette was pregnant with his child.

My mother was devastated. King Charles is the oldest son of the oldest son of Oberian. We are still working to repair the damage from the war of the roaches. We cannot afford our family name to be disgraced by a child born of a common citizen who is, in their eyes, beneath our family. I don't know if I agree with this argument, but it is the will of our King. Who am I to stand against it?

Before my sister could start to show in the belly, my father passed. We had to wait on a decision for the days of mourning and my coronation. I am now Queen of Enchenda. My mother, the former holder of the title, has no royal blood. She had no choice but to hand off the title gracefully, but she is not happy to be done with it.

In secret, she continued to try and make decisions and answer scrolls addressed to the Queen of Enchenda. She would tell me to shut my mouth at dinner and would often take the seat at the head of the table where my father used to sit. I wondered, during those days, if she had always been cruel or if this was something grief had wrought upon her. I fear I will never have that answer.

My mother did, however, allow Suzette to remain in our home during her entire pregnancy. She forbade me to mention the pregnancy to the council. A request I'm sorry to admit I accepted wholeheartedly. I now wish I had told them because it may have prevented that which came to pass.

On the day my sister went into labor, my mother had every servant sent from our home. She brought my sister to a back bedroom and made me come to assist with the birth. I know nothing of medicine and bringing children into the world but somehow we were able to get it done. Suzette was alive and well and the baby, a beautiful little chubby girl, came into the world drawing breath.

I am sure of that.

As sure as I am that my mother did something to that child in the moments following.

She will not admit it, of course. The way she tells the tale the baby called Margarite was born without the ability to draw breath. She told Suzette that the baby never stood a chance. That it died before it was even of the world.

Reader, I don't believe that. I saw the little chest rise and fall. I saw it more than once before my mother bent low in front of my vision and smothered that child.

After that, I am not sure whether Suzette left of her own accord or whether my mother banished her from our home. I could not blame her if it was the first. If I were not needed to hold the title for this realm, I would do the same. As it is, I fear for my life. My mother knows I alone was in that room with her to witness what she did. When I spread this news she will know exactly where it has come from and she will come for me. I may be Queen but that woman has more power and influence than I do.

I will speak with my Aunt Salen. Enchenda must be prepared. Enchenda must have a Queen. Salen must be prepared to step up if something happens to me.

I am going to the council today but they may side with my mother and bury this story. If you are reading this, you must help me set their truths straight.

Suzette had a loving relationship but she was not

allowed to marry. The child, technically born out of wedlock, was not born out of a loving relationship. She deserved a chance to live a full life.

That child, Margarite, was murdered by my mother the former Queen of Enchenda.

Enchenda is supposed to be great and humble, honoring the image of my grandfather. We are supposed to help the council remember that being too proud can lead to your downfall. We must rise above this cruelty and set it right. I fear what will happen to our future generations if we continue to hide things like this.

We must be better, Enchenda.

This scroll was found during the reign of Queen Sawchett of Enchenda in an abandoned room of the royal family home. My research as updater for Enchenda shows the lineage did pass from Selena to her surviving Aunt, Salen. This scroll gives us an interesting reason that may have been.

The names Suzette and Margarite were penned on the royal tree in Enchenda but blocked out. During the reign of Queen Eselda, they were uncovered for all to see. During the reign of Queen Sawchett, the names were added to the complete tree in the council building in the center of the Kingdom of Fraun.

My research has been unable to determine whether the tale in this scroll is accurate, but I have found nothing to dispute it. -Tutor

Running From the Kingdom

Lili opens the door to the shop in the center of Renchenda and tries to enter the room quickly, keeping the cold outdoor air from following her in. A shiver dances down her arms despite her best effort. Lili takes stock of the shop she's been in only once before. Again, a fire burns in the grate. The temperature here is considerably higher than that of the outside air. The man behind the counter, who Lili assumes is the historian on duty, is bent low over a large scroll. She takes a few tentative steps in his direction and he looks up. "Can I help you find anything today?" he asks.

"No. I'm actually here for a second interview," Lili answers. She keeps the cloak pulled tight around her middle. The fire makes the cloak unnecessary but she'd rather keep her secret a bit longer. She needs this job to be able to earn her keep in Renchenda and trade commodities for housing and food. One can never tell how a secret like this will cloud someone's judgment and, therefore, the chance of earning a job like this one.

"Ah, that'll make you Lili. Come on over here. You previously met my wife. She spoke very highly of your organizational and speaking skills." He rolls up the scroll he was reading and reaches for another one behind him. Then he comes out from behind the little counter and offers Lili his hand for a quick shake, which she complies with. "We just have the matter of the written portion of your interview to conduct. We like to be sure all of our historians can read and write before we bring them in. This is a formality at this point, you understand."

She does. She understands that Renchenda wants to know that you are capable of reading anything on any scroll at any time before they ask you to ignore parts of the history of the realm that may be documented on the scrolls you are cataloging. She resists the urge to roll her eyes and reminds herself, again, that she needs this job. Renchenda treats citizens well if they feel they are productive members of society. She must be contributing to society in order to receive her benefits. She knows this. She can do this. "Not a problem," she says. "Do you have a table I can work at and a writing utensil I can borrow?"

He hands her the scroll and a quill. Once they are

transferred to her hand he gestures to a table and chair off to the side of the shop. The table is nestled in among two shelves each full of scrolls. There is a small candle resting on the table, providing enough light for her to work by. She wonders if the candle is always there. It seems rather dangerous to have an open flame so near to all the scrolls and parchments they must go through at a historian's office. But that is not her place so she keeps this question to herself.

She drops into the chair and unrolls the scroll, which appears to have about ten questions on it. She lets go of the cloak now that she is seated facing away from the historian, hoping the desk will help maintain her secret. Then, she gets to work.

Lili notices the first few questions are easy ones and fires off their answers quickly in her slightly slanted and careful handwriting.

<u>Name the rulers of the realms in Fraun.</u>

King Todd of Sarcheda

King Gregario of Enchenda

King Mick of Farcheda

King Larecio of Marchenda

Queen Aine of Renchenda

<u>Name the traits and colors associated with the realms in Fraun.</u>

Sarcheda embodies strength and wears red.

Enchenda embodies humility and wears green.

Farcheda embodies speed and wears blue.

Marchenda embodies mirth and wears yellow.

Renchenda embodies wisdom and wears orange.

The third question, although simple enough, requires Lili to access information held way back in her brain and dig for the answer. Luckily, she looked over her old schooling materials in preparation for this interview today. This is not the kind of information she normally remembers quickly.

<u>Name the rulers in Fraun history who have held the position of First Realm.</u>

King Enchenda the first ruler of Enchenda

King Charles of Enchenda

King Marcher of Marchenda

King Franthe of Marchenda

King Freth of Renchenda

Queen Alep of Renchenda

King Stan of Sarcheda

King Todd of Sarcheda

She almost forgets Queen Alep, who lost the first realm seat simply for what can only be described as misogyny. At least that's the way Lili feels. Look at the list. Alep is the only one on the list with the word Queen in her title instead of King and she held the position of ruler of the first realm for the shortest amount of time. In the rest of history, the royals lost their seat for lack of heirs, suspicious activity, arguing unfavorably in council, or even for asking to step down. But Queen Alep had children and a spouse. She was well prepared to serve that council. The way the historians recorded it seems logical, but Lili wonders what is not being said in those lines.

The fourth question piques her interest. She is careful to word her answers in a way that will not offend anyone, conscious that she is putting this in writing.

<u>Name a weakness associated with each realm of Fraun.</u>

In Sarcheda, they believe women to be weaker than men.

In Enchenda, they devalue the individual in favor of the whole.

In Farcheda, they rush to conclusions often without weighing all evidence.

In Marchenda, they often focus on individual incidents instead of the bigger picture.

In Rechenda, they often forget to enjoy experiences and live in the moment.

She feels like the answers are simple enough for her purpose today, although incomplete. Lili could write volumes on why it is unwise to be raised in the way they are here, separate from each other and without complete lessons on everything. She has a better education than many, she knows, because she was raised in Renchenda. But she doesn't believe this is enough. A child should be more well-rounded than even she has had the chance to be.

She reaches below the little table and rubs her

stomach. Again, she begins to wonder if this is the right decision. Should she be raising her baby here? He or she will be here soon and Lili just isn't sure this is the right place for them anymore.

She can't worry about that now. Now, she needs a job to trade her skills for food. She needs to finish this questionnaire.

<u>Name a profession common in each realm of Fraun.</u>

Lili rolls her eyes. All of the professions happen in all of the realms. She can't imagine Enchenda not having a historian of their own, for example. If you aren't allowing the citizens to interact with each other often and share the responsibilities, they must each have their own. But this is not what she is expected to write and she knows it. She will give examples of jobs that she expects she would easily be able to find if she lived in those realms.

Sarcheda-builder

Enchenda-merchant

Farcheda-weaver

Marchenda-farmer

Renchenda-teacher

<u>In Fraun, balance is key. How does our council demonstrate balance?</u>

Lili is certain she cannot simply write that they don't. She hasn't been to the council room but it is obvious they don't care about that. Why else would you have each realm care for themselves and look after themselves? She rubs her stomach again and wonders why she is doing this.

Fraun is idealistic, she'll give them that. But it is a dream her parents had. It is a dream her grandparents had. It is not her dream. She doesn't want to be praised for her brain and nothing else. She doesn't want to practice being wise above being humble. This isn't the answer.

She pushes back from the table and lets the scroll roll back up.

"Finished already?" the man asks, his voice tinged with shock.

"I've changed my mind," Lili answers. "I don't think this position would be a good fit for me."

"Were the questions too difficult?" he asks, tipping his head a little to the side as if he is suddenly feeling sorry for the young Fraunian.

Lili laughs. "Not at all. I think I just realized that this isn't what I want for my life." She reaches down and pulls the cloak open, revealing the swollen stomach full of life. "It's not what I want for our lives."

The historian does not hide his shock well. Instead, he lets it show on his entire face. "What do you plan to do for work with an infant at home?" he asks. "Surely you plan to contribute."

"Don't worry about me," she says. "We will be perfectly fine."

Lili leaves through the same door she entered but her feet carry her in another direction entirely. She walks across the quiet streets past homes buttoned up against the cold. She moves without a purpose, headed vaguely in the direction of the woods. She's heard talk of people leaving Fraun. People who intend to start a new group of Scouts, wandering the expanse of the world beyond the border. Surely there are no expectations there of things she can or cannot teach her child.

Perhaps that is her answer.

At the edge of Renchenda, she spies a group of young men trimming branches from trees. "Excuse me," she calls. The men turn and she offers a smile. "I'm wondering if any of you are familiar with the rumors of the scout troop that has formed nearby. Perhaps you can tell me where to find them?"

Most of the men laugh but one, a short one with a kind face, takes a step toward Lili. "Talk to the roaches," he whispers. Before she can ask any follow-up questions or process fully what he has said, he is back with the group, laughing as if he agreed with the joke the entire time. Lili wonders for just a second if she heard him right but she dares not to ask again.

Instead, she nods once at the group and leaves. This time she is looking for the many-legged creatures who share her realm. She is looking for a roach.

She doesn't have to look long before she finds one. She makes noise as she approaches so as not to shock the creature. "I was told to ask you if you know where I can find the group that resides outside of Fraun," she says. "Can you point me to someone who may know where to go?"

"I can do better than that," the roach says. "I can take you when you are ready. I know just the group."

"You can take me," Lili repeats. "How exactly does that work?"

A sound that may be a laugh comes from the creature. "You climb aboard my back with one foot on either side of my body. You can hold on to the top of my exoskeleton if you wish. Then I walk as normal except that you travel with me. With any luck, I will remember that you are up there and drop you off at your destination without scurrying right past it."

"You would do that for me?" Lili squints her eyes in confusion. "You don't know anything about me. What makes you so sure that you can trust me to ride safely without hurting you? I would imagine I am a bit heavier than you. Plus," she pulls back her cloak, again revealing the baby she has worked so hard to contain from society until this point. "I'm also carrying a child, which makes the weight even greater."

The roach's antennae move around her as if trying to gauge her size. "That shouldn't be a problem. My name is Gee. I am strong enough to handle the weight of someone your size and an infant. You travel home and get your affairs in order. When do you think you'll be ready for such a journey?"

Lili weighs her options. There is no one left for her in Fraun, now that her parents and her husband are gone. The people of Renchenda are kind enough and no one would argue that they are caring. But in the lunar cycles since the fire, she has become more and more certain that the kingdom where she was raised is not perfect. Her choices, it appears, are to raise her child in imperfection or to fight to change the system. Lili isn't sure she has it in her to fight. Not when the changes needed are so vast. Not when running is an option. "I would very much like to be quick about it," she answers. "Thank you. By the way, I am Lili and I appreciate you very much, Gee. How about if we agree I will be back in a fortnight with a small bag of things I need? Does that work for you?"

"I shall see you then," Gee says.

Lili returns home, already feeling lighter with a plan in place. It is not the plan she had a lunar cycle ago, but things change.

During the fortnight, Lili has many opportunities to change her mind. Instead, she finds herself praising her choice. When, for example, she gives away many of the belongings she will not be needing to neighbors and no one asks her why she is getting rid of her things, she realizes she won't be missed here. When she heads to the grocer to trade a few hours of labor for some food for the evening and is turned away because of the infant growing in her stomach and told to "send her husband to do the work while she rests her feet", she knows she will also not miss them.

When the baby comes into the world just as the sun is rising for the seventh time since she decided to leave Fraun and she holds him in her arms for the first time, all doubts about her choice leave her. This new child, her boy, will grow up better and stronger than Lili herself was ever allowed to be because he will grow up away from the restrictions of the kingdom. When the kind neighbor who helped her deliver the child asks his name, Lili takes inspiration from the count of days and her deceased husband's name. She combines seven with Siege and tells the woman the child's name will be Sieven.

Late afternoon of the traveling day arrives and Lili meets Gee at the same location on the edge of Renchenda. She has a small bag of clothing and food but her biggest parcel is the blanket-wrapped Sieven she is holding in front of her. She nods at Gee. "Are you ready for the journey?" she asks.

"I am. Are you?"

"We are." She climbs aboard the back of the creature as she was instructed half a lunar cycle ago. His back is smooth and hard, not unlike the shells of the nuts that fall from the trees on the outskirts of town. Through her layers of clothing, she can feel the warmth of the creature radiate. "How long is the ride?" she asks.

"Not long. The sun will likely finish its journey across the sky and drop below where we can see but we should arrive with the group shortly after that. That is unless you are not comfortable traveling at night."

There is a part of her that knows this is likely a huge mistake. She has told no one where she is going. Should something go wrong, no one in Fraun would know where to find her.

But she also knows that if she goes back to that house she will find a reason to stay. The last thing she wants is for three annuals to pass while she is still in the same place dreaming of something different. She uncovers Sieven's little face and smiles down at him. Again, she knows this is the right decision and the time needs to be now before Sieven can begin to form attachments to this place. "I'm fine with traveling at night. Let's go."

As if he can sense that she might change her mind if given the chance, Gee sets off further into the forest.

For the first half of the ride, Lili simply enjoys the change that comes with being outside the boundaries of the kingdom where she has spent her entire life. The trees are denser here and the noises are different. Gone are the sounds of Fraunians and the noises they bring into the world. In its place, she hears scurrying feet, birds, and other noises that must belong to animals she is not familiar with. "If you don't mind my asking, where exactly do you live?" Lili asks her companion. "Do you live inside of Fraun?"

"No, although some of my kind certainly do." He speaks slower now, breathing heavily between the words. "I live in the forest near where you met up with me. We are travelers by nature and the radius I go each day is rather large. I never quite understood how you in the kingdom are content to stay in one place most days. Are you one of the ones who has never left before?" he asks.

"I am. This is my first time outside of Fraun."

"And what do you think of the world?" he asks.

Lili leans her head back to look up at the sky peeking through the treetops. The fresh air rushes by her face, smelling sweet and clean. A smile takes over her face. "I love it," she answers. "I already feel like the world is free here. I didn't even realize how heavy the rules of Fraun felt on my shoulders until I came out here with you and took them off." She looks down at the roach. "Thank you for being here to help me do it. I think I would have talked myself out of it if I had waited much longer."

"You are welcome."

The second half of the ride seems to take a lot longer. Lili finds her thighs hurt from being at this new angle. Her bottom hurts from where it sits on the unforgiving surface of the creature. Her arms tire from supporting the weight of the infant. Her nose has gone cold with the passing wind and now that the sun is setting it is becoming harder to see what else may be lurking in the shadows. In Fraun she was safe from animals that may wish to do her harm. They're taught from a young age that creatures are a danger to them. Not because they are inherently evil but because, to them, Fraunians are a convenient size for snacking or stepping on accidentally. It is much the same way the creatures would have been treated by the giants, she assumes. When you are so much larger than another being, it becomes difficult to think of them as equal to you in ways not related to size. Likely this forest is teaming with creatures that could do her harm. That makes her nervous.

"Do you travel this way often?" Lili asks. "Aren't there creatures out here that would harm you?"

"We are safe," Gee answers, his breath even more labored than before. "I am moving too quickly for most of them. It is only birds that would be a risk to us here and very few of the kind you would see out here are skilled enough to pose a threat."

"That is good to know." She wants to ask more about the group they are heading to but feels guilty whenever she asks questions that require him to speak in sentences to answer her. She has heard talk of a few groups calling themselves Scouts. Some sound almost like employees of the kingdom, bringing materials back to them when they require them. Some stay far away from the kingdom, having no contact. She wonders what kind of group she has gotten herself into. Is it possible they will have rules like those she left behind? What would she do then? She supposes she would merely find herself another kind roach to take her back to Fraun. If she can make her decision within a fortnight it's likely no one will even notice she has been gone.

The darkness fully falls now out in this area away from civilization and cloaked in trees that keep moonlight from reaching them. Lili finds very little difference between the dark of night with her eyes open and the dark behind her eyelids when they are closed. A sleepy feeling begins to take over her limbs. She feels herself drifting off, catching her head falling toward her chest time and time again. She wonders how Gee manages to find the route in the darkness.

"We are approaching," Gee says. "I will need to stop soon and give them a chance to see us coming. They are kind but they are not stupid. We should not sneak into their camp unannounced."

When she opens her eyes, she can see faint flickers of light in the trees ahead. For some reason, this sends Lili's heart racing. Maybe this was a mistake. Should she tell Gee to drop her right here? Can she camp for the night alone and head back in the morning? But, of course, that would be foolish. If there are animals that can cause her harm out here they would be more likely to attack her alone when she is defenseless.

Beneath her, she feels Gee's momentum come to a stop. She pulls her right leg up, her hip screaming in protest from being moved, and drops off the left side of the roach. Her legs are wobbling unsteadily underneath her. There are flares of pain all up and down her legs, she takes a moment to rub them with her free hand. She is starting to understand why riding on roaches is not something Fraunians do regularly. This is torture.

"Can I help you find someone?" a voice calls.

Lili stands up straight and finds a tall man with broad shoulders standing in the clearing before her, a torch in his hand illuminating his body and the area around him. His clothing would be typical for a Fraunian, clearly repurposed and slightly too large for him but comfortable and practical. It does, however, seem to intentionally avoid the five colors associated with the realms of Fraun. This clothing looks like it may have been colored using tree bark. It is mostly brown. "I am Lili," she calls. "I am traveling with my infant son, Sieven. I am from Renchenda and I was hoping you could help me learn to be on my own." The explanation is poor, she knows, but it is strange to be yelling across a small clearing at a man she has never met before. Plus, her legs are still hurting in so many areas.

"Come this way into the light," he calls. "Let's have a chat."

Lili takes a few wobbly and painful steps closer to the man. She stops and turns back to find Gee has not moved. "You go ahead," he says. "I have business to attend to with some of my kin out here. Good luck, girl."

"Thank you," Lili calls. "You were very helpful."

"My kind always are. Remember that." He scurries off into the darkness of the forest before she can promise that she will. Her attention turns back to the man. She watches him as she draws closer. She realizes that he must be close to her age. For a beat she is surprised. How is someone her age so much more confident and prepared for their future? How is it he came to be here?

When she is standing in front of him she holds her hand out as she has been taught. "Thank you for agreeing to speak with me," she says.

"I'm Franc. My wife and I were also once of Fraun and we welcome you if your intentions are good. Do you have any weapons or anything on you that I should be worried about?"

Lili shakes her head vehemently. "Absolutely not. I have some clothing in the bag I carry and the infant in my arms. Nothing else. Honestly, I'm starting to wonder if I haven't made a huge mistake."

"Why would you worry about that? You haven't done anything permanent yet. You're here visiting a couple of kind people. Come in, have a seat around the fire, and meet Carlina. You can start your worrying in the morning when the decision begins to get more real. Tonight, you're a guest." Franc turns and walks from the clearing, his footsteps heavy.

Lili, afraid of the full darkness that will be left

behind in the wake of his torch leaving, hurries to follow him. They walk through a corridor of trees for a few steps before Lili notices a much larger light coming from somewhere before him. After a few more steps, another clearing emerges. This one is ringed around a decent-sized campfire. Three fabric houses of some kind line the outer area of the clearing at the edge of the trees. In front of the fire, a woman with long straight hair sits on a log with a bit of sewing in her lap.

"It was a roach bringing another defect of Renchenda," Franc calls to the group. "She says her name is Lili and she's brought an infant with her."

The woman drops the sewing and stands in one quick motion. "An infant? Oh, let me see." She crosses the clearing quickly and offers Lili a smile before pulling the blanket back from Sieven's sleeping face. "What a precious little miracle. What's the name?"

"He is called Sieven," Lili answers.

"Hello, Sieven," the woman says to the baby. Finally, she turns her attention to Lili. "And hello to you as well, Lili. I am Carlina and this is my husband, Franc." She gestures to the man Lili has already met. "Are you shunned from the Fraun or leaving of your own accord?" she asks.

Lili likes the forward nature of the question right away. She can think of many situations that would result in Renchenda or other realms of Fraun turning her away for having this child. But that is not her situation. "I left of my own accord. The kingdom may not be perfect but I cannot imagine they would punish a widow for having her husband's child after his death. Sieven has earned me no scorn. I only wish to bring him up in a different environment. One that is more focused on letting him learn who he truly is instead of fitting him into a box they want him for."

"What if who he truly is turns out to be someone who wants to be raised inside that box?" Franc asks.

Lili finds she hadn't considered that. What if she goes to all this trouble to leave her life behind only to have her son grow up and run back to it? She takes a beat to consider it. "It worked for me and it would work for him if that is what he decides. But right now it just isn't right for us."

"Wise words," Carlina says. "You were of Renchenda, weren't you?"

Lili smiles. "Am I that obvious?"

Carlina turns back toward the fire. "Come, join us. I made some stew a bit ago and it's still warm." She returns to her seat by the fire and gestures to a pot on the edge of the pit. Then she reaches down and picks up her sewing. "Come on, put your stuff down and join me."

Lili takes the second prompt and moves. She drops her bag beside another log and sits. "Do you have something I can put the stew in?"

"Already on it," Franc says, appearing at her elbow

with a bowl. He reaches for the pot, removes the lid, and scoops some of the warm mixture into the bowl. He offers it to Lili. "Would you like to set the boy down while you eat?" he asks.

"Oh, no. I'll take him." Again Carlina's sewing finds itself in a heap at her feet as her arms reach for Lili. "Please let me take him. I can't have children, they tell me. This is my chance to get close to one."

Lili smiles and hands Sieven to the woman. She watches as both of them get comfortable with the snuggled posture before she takes the bowl from Franc and begins eating. She tries to eat slowly and remain composed but finds that her stomach is craving the food. The bowl is empty before she really has time to process the action.

"How old are you?" Franc asks. "If you don't mind my asking."

"I don't mind at all," Lili answers. "I am twenty-two annuals. You?"

"I'm twenty-three and my wife here is the baby of our group at barely twenty."

Carlina coos like a bird in Sieven's face. "I'm not the baby anymore, am I little Sieven? No, you have that title, you beautiful little miracle."

Lili notices she feels comfortable here like she hasn't felt comfortable anywhere in a long time. Maybe it's the fire, or the stew, or the kind people. Maybe it's simply being outside of the kingdom on her own for the first time in her life. Whatever it is, she knows she feels more at home than she has since the fire. She wants to be here. She wants to be a part of this. "What is your purpose with this group?" she asks. "What do you call yourselves?"

"We call ourselves scouts," Franc answers. "For lack of a better name. We want to see what else is out in the world. We knew there had to be more than what we were exposed to in Fraun."

Carlina looks up from the baby's face. "We didn't need all the pressures of life there in your kingdom," she explains. "Sometimes, even though we had plenty of space, it just felt too constricting. We needed to breathe." She takes a deep breath of the air and Lili finds herself copying the motion, filling her lungs with the sweet smell of fresh air.

"I know exactly what you mean," Lili says. "Will you bring items that could be useful to the kingdoms back? I've heard some groups do that while others bear a sort of ill will for the citizens and the royalty."

"No ill will here," Franc says. "We have no hard feelings. If we find something useful, we'll bring it. I left some family behind there. This was never about leaving the Fraun for us."

"Not exclusively that, anyway," Carlina adds.

"Right, we don't mean them any harm or anything," Franc says.

"It just wasn't for us," Carlina finishes. "Out here in

the wilderness with our fire and each other, that's us."

Lili suddenly feels like she could cry but it would be happy tears. "I think," she says, "I'm finally home. If you'll have us, of course."

Carlina smiles down at the infant again. "You're already family, honey."

Memories from Charlotte

The woman who now thinks of herself as an old woman paces her home. When she woke up this morning her long hair was grey. Completely grey. Not going grey, not almost grey, grey. She knows what that means in Fraun. That means she is going to die. It's something everyone knows from the moment they are born but it's not something you confront until you have to. It's scary for anyone, knowing that the final day is coming. You have to try and wrap things up, tie off the loose ends, say the things that you need to say.

For her, it's worse than that. She has to decide what secrets to take to her grave.

She turns and looks behind her at the small child playing on the floor. The child that never should have been. The child is four annuals now. Soon, she will be speaking. She will need to go to school. The school may ask questions about her that the woman will find hard to answer. The girl will need to be taught to say "she is my Aunt" if anyone asks. It's easier that way. But what if she slips up?

There is another option, the woman knows. She could ask for a tutor. Someone who can come to the house and give the girl lessons. It's practically unheard of for someone of common blood. Of course … no, she stops herself before she can even finish the thought. She is so used to keeping this secret that she can't even let herself think the thought fully.

She reaches her hand down to the toddler. "C'mon, let's go outside." Some parents in Fraun forget to talk to their small children simply because they cannot talk back. But her husband was adamant that they speak frequently with the child. She should hear the language often so that she's not surprised to find she has some words already when she's capable of speech, he used to say. Oh, how she misses him. She misses waking up in the morning to find his face beside her. She misses the way he would give her pointed looks over the table when something happened that he found ridiculous or silly. She misses the closeness that only comes with sharing your life and your secrets with another.

The girl stands and walks across the house to the

door. There, she stops and looks behind her. The woman almost laughs. This is a look that will surely accompany cross words when the girl is older. She will chide her mother for taking too long or for walking too slowly.

But no, of course, that's not right. She will have to call the woman Aunt, never Mother. Her shoulders sag and she sighs. Maybe having this child was not a good idea after all. What has she done?

Outside, the woman finds a neighbor has left her a basket of green beans. She sits on the front stoop and begins snapping the ends of the beans, making a small pile beside her. The girl rushes to the grass across from the house and spins in circles, throwing her arms out to either side. The woman smiles at her.

Across the grass and over the girl's head, she spies the man she never thought she'd see again. This is a story she never let herself think about. Now, in honor of the fact that her hair has gone grey this morning, she will let herself remember.

"It's a boy." The medicine woman stands beside the bed, holding the baby in her hands. "Do you want to hold him?"

Charlotte looks beside her to where Den is kneeling. "Should I?" she asks. The baby came from her. It's the baby they never should have made. The baby could cause a lot of chaos for Enchenda. This baby should not be here, he should never have been. In the last few annuals, Charlotte has spent a lot of time digging into the story her mother told her. She was looking for proof that it was a lie. She hoped it was.

Instead, she and Den learned that everything she had been told was true. Her mother had a love affair with the then-prince of Enchenda. But he married another woman, a woman who became Queen. Charlotte, although she was raised as a commoner, is royal blood. Royal blood should be charted by the council. It should be recorded on the wall. It should not be swaddled in a small blanket, born in secret, and about to be secreted away to another realm to grow up alone, without parents.

Tears slip down her cheeks unchecked. "If you let me hold him, I will never let him go," she admits. "I can't. I can't give him up."

"You can't keep him," Den whispers. "Imagine what Gregario would do if he found out."

"He can raise him." Charlotte puts her arms behind her and sits up. "They need an heir. The boy has royal blood. We'll just give him to Greg. Then I can see him—"

Den interrupts her by laying a hand on her arm and giving her a look that can only be described as pained. "We don't know what he would say if we presented the idea. I'm worried it would be dangerous for you. Plus, if you're honest, how hard would it be to see the child be raised as a prince? Is that really what you want?"

"No," she admits. "But I don't know if I can let him go."

"He's going to a good home. You found the family in Farcheda yourself. They're good people. They'll care for him."

In the end, Charlotte goes along with the plan. She does hold the baby. She has clear memories of looking into those eyes and feeling the tug of maternal love that would forever connect her to the boy. She remembers calling him only "boy" because she didn't know what they would name him. She remembers crying when she had to hand him to the medicine woman to drop off with his new family. She remembers crying for days. She knew it was the right thing to do but that didn't make it easy.

She doesn't remember the exact moment when she started heading to the boys' school in the center of Enchenda where they take in parentless Fraunians. Once, Den caught her there. He was standing right on the stoop of the house and saw her come out of the doorway. He stomped his way across the square and got right in her face. "What are you doing?"

"I just have a feeling," she told him. "The boy is going to come back here. It's something I can't explain."

"You can't be here. What will people think?"

"They'll think what we tell them. They'll think we can't have children. It's fine."

It was not fine. It was slowly growing between them every day and night. Charlotte would dream of the baby, dream of seeing him again. In her dreams, he was growing long hair, smiling, and laughing. He was talking. He was impressing his teachers and learning his lessons. But always, in her dreams, he was coming home at night to her house.

Then Den was fired. It should never have happened. Den was in the garden, taking a break from tutoring the young princess when Queen Rubina came out and took a seat. According to Den, they were merely having a conversation. Charlotte is sure there must have been more to the story, things he was unwilling to tell even her. In the end, Den had been let go from his position. Weirder still, Queen Rubina was not seen again. It was half a fortnight before King Gregario announced her untimely death. But something about that did not feel right. Charlotte couldn't explain what it was. She only knew that Den felt it too. He was jumpy and worried about everything. He kept the curtains closed when they were home.

They took a vacation, something small that would get them out of Enchenda and away from the memories. Charlotte had begun to visit the boys' home every other sun. At night, she was constantly dreaming about the boy. So it was easy to suggest they vacation in Farcheda. Maybe, she thought, she'd find the boy from her dreams. Surely her heart would recognize him immediately.

Den changed while they were in Farcheda for the fortnight. He was happy again, lighter. They enjoyed dinners amongst people who didn't know he had been fired while tutoring the princess. They didn't know anything about these people and that turned out to be perfect. It was on this vacation that Sawchett was conceived. In a moment of happiness, they pretended to be the kind of couple who could simply have children. She wasn't sorry for that, merely sorry that she couldn't give the girl the childhood she deserved.

Charlotte remembers returning from the vacation so clearly. At the border of Enchenda, she kissed her husband and squeezed his hand where it was wrapped around hers. "I'm going to the grocer," he said. "I'll meet you at home."

"Perfect." She didn't tell him she was going to the boys' home.

Perhaps he already knew. When she was ten steps from the home the front door opened and three boys came out, laughing. The sun seemed to shine brighter on one, an average-sized boy with hair falling in his eyes. He reached up and brushed it out of his face and Charlotte's heart threatened to leap from her chest. This was the boy she had dreamed of.

She crossed the distance between them faster than she should have been capable of. "Excuse me," she greeted him. She had the presence of mind to smile at all three boys in turn, lest they think her strange. "Are you boys new here?"

"Just arrived," the boy answered. "I've been exploring the realms. I was raised in Renchenda but I want to see all of Fraun."

"Renchenda? You look like a baby I knew of a family from Farcheda. But that's silly, of course, who looks like a baby?"

"I was born in Farcheda," the boy offered. "I'm Tutor."

"Tutor," she repeats, the name feeling perfectly shaped on her tongue. This was the boy, she was sure of it.

Before the sun set that day, Charlotte had convinced the boy to stay with her and Den while he was in Enchenda until he found something more permanent. Den must have realized who he was as well because there was no argument on the topic.

Instead, Den had taught the boy his craft. He'd made sure the boy knew everything about royal blood and tutoring. He'd sent him to the home of the king with everything he needed to take the job his birth father had been let go from.

One night Den came to her once Sawchett was asleep. Tutor was out with a few of the friends he had made, she recalls. Den had plopped heavily into the chair across from her, his face a mask of seriousness. She knew that look. He had something he wanted to tell her. "What is it?" she prompted. "Let's not waste time dancing around whatever it is. Let's deal with it."

"I want to tell Tutor the truth."

Whatever she had been expecting him to say, that was not it. It had shocked her completely. She sat back in the chair, unable to come up with any words to say or any questions to ask him. In the void left by her silence, Den rushed on. "I have been bonding with him, we're getting along wonderfully. But I'm not going to last forever." He reached his hand up then, she recalls, and brushed it back through his grey hair almost automatically. He had been grey at this point for about three annuals, she knew. It was always easy to calculate because Sawchett had been born shortly after he awoke to a head of grey hair. If the medicine men and women of Fraun were right, and they usually were, Den only had a few annuals left. "I want to go knowing that my son is becoming a better person than I was. I want him to know he was loved. I want him to know who I am."

"He knows we are the people who brought him into our home. He knows we love him."

"He deserves the truth, Charlotte."

She doesn't remember how long it took him to convince her or what the final argument was that sold her on the plan. She only remembers that when Tutor came home that night, a little tipsy from something he and his friends had been drinking, they all sat at that table together and Tutor listened to the story. She didn't tell him everything. She merely told him that she and Den were already married when he was conceived. They loved each other, and him, very much. But they weren't ready to be parents. They couldn't afford to raise children. They wanted him to have the very best. She told him they had hand-selected the family in Farcheda.

Everything she told him that day was true, she tells herself. So it's alright that it was missing a huge chunk of the puzzle.

She sighs now, watching Tutor run his errands at various shops around the square. He'll never know. Den has died and now Charlotte will die and Tutor will never know. He'll never know the blood that runs in his veins and those of his baby sister is as royal as the girl he tutors. He'll never know and that is the worst secret of her life.

She stands up from the stoop, her brain seizing on an idea. She reaches down and grabs Sawchett, plopping her on one hip even as her feet are carrying her across the square. "Tutor," she calls.

He stops, turning and looking for her. He smiles when he finds her and offers a wave. "Good morning, Charlotte. How are you today?"

She doesn't see him often enough anymore. He has moved out of her home, choosing instead to live in a smaller place nearby. He still visits, sometimes having dinner with her and Sawchett. But she knows he is growing older and ready to make a life of his own that doesn't involve her. If she's honest with herself, she knows he has begun putting space between them since he learned of what she did when he was a baby. It was hard for him to accept the truth. He has told her that he forgives her for what she had to do. She's glad about that. He wants to be involved in their lives, he wants to know Sawchett and have a relationship with her, but he also doesn't fully understand everything. They had asked him to keep this little secret but they couldn't tell him why, of course. This means he doesn't understand why he can't say he's their son or call Sawchett his sister. It puts a wall between them and Charlotte hates that wall. But there is no other way.

"I have a proposition for you," she says now. "Do you have a minute?"

Tutor's eyes track up to the sun. "I have a bit. What can I do for you?"

Charlotte adjusts Sawchett on her hip, drawing Tutor's eyes down to the child. Charlotte watches his face soften and he smiles, reaching for the girl. Sawchett reaches her hand out toward him as well, grasping a few of his fingers in her smaller fist. "Good morning, little one," he coos. He makes no move to pull his hand from her.

"Actually, it's about Sawchett here," Charlotte says. This earns her the full attention of the son she cannot claim in public. His eyes widen in surprise and he stares at her, expectant. "She will be five annuals soon and that requires her formal education to begin. I was thinking, perhaps, that our strange situation would prove a little difficult to explain to a curious teacher who means well. I was thinking, maybe, of hiring her a tutor who can deliver her education in a more private setting."

"You have nothing to trade for that kind of expense," Tutor says.

He's not wrong, of course. Now that Den has passed and Charlotte has to care for the household herself, commodities are limited. She can trade sewing and labor for food enough for the child, but it consumes much of her time. There is rarely any time left for taking on more jobs that might repay a tutor. There is a reason most common citizens use the school. "I would be eternally grateful to the person who undertakes this sort of responsibility. It would be best for Sawchett, of course. I will find a way to repay them."

"Charlotte, be plain. Are you asking me to pay for Sawchett's training?"

Charlotte shakes her head. "For Fraun's sake, no. I thought I was being less subtle than I am, evidently. I was asking you to consider handling her education."

Tutor's shoulder's relax as if that answer is much better than what he was considering. He chuckles. "Oh, that's much better. I can probably work something out." He squeezes Sawchett's hand before dropping it. Then he leans down and kisses the child on her forehead. "We'll get you good training, I promise," he says. Then, to Charlotte. "Let me work on the schedule and see what I can do. I'll be in touch."

She watches him walk away in the direction of the royal family home. She thinks, again, of how much easier it would be to talk with him if he just knew everything. If he knew the reason Sawchett cannot go to school was that she has royal blood. If he knew that Gregario, the king he praises, was the reason his birth father was fired from his job. If he knew, as the first of his generation born in Enchenda with royal blood, he would have more rights to that throne than the princess he tutors. If he knew all that, he would understand.

She sighs.

He will never know all that. She cannot do that to Gregario. Not because of the king he is now, she has no respect for that title. But for the man he was. For the man she thought he would be. That man deserves a chance to raise his daughter the way he envisioned and telling the truth of Tutor's birth would change everything.

The following are excerpts from the personal scrolls of Queen Aine of Renchenda.

Aine, the Logical

13th Annual, 3rd Lunar Cycle, 5 Suns past Quarter Moon

My brother took my mother from me. It's the most illogical thought I have and yet it is also the strongest thought I have. Before my brother was born I had a mother who cared for me. She brushed my hair, she talked to me about real life, and she helped me understand the world outside the heavy burden of studies my realm puts on me.

Then, my brother was born. One moment she was here, belly swollen with new life. The next moment, she was gone and I only had that screaming baby in her place. So, although I know the logic behind it and know that my mother's time was at an end, I also know that my brother took my mother from me just by being born.

20th Annual, 1st Lunar Cycle, 3 Suns past Full Moon

It is time I start keeping personal scrolls. Tonight I went down for dinner, intending to grab my food and retreat to the library as always. I even had my plan all set. I've been studying the rule of King Marcher, the former King of Farcheda. He was King from a young age. During his reign, his realm got to be the first realm, which is a big deal. So, when I came down to the dining room, I was ready to explain my research and take my food to the library. Father is the king of wisdom, of course. There's nothing he enjoys more than scrolls and discussing them.

Instead, he made me stay. When I asked for permission to leave the room he said something like "Actually, there's something we must discuss." He commanded me to sit. He doesn't usually command things. He suggests them, and he recites appropriate research, but he does not command anything.

I sat at the table, directly across from Thometh who was looking obnoxiously immature with his tongue sticking out of his mouth in what I assume was intended to be a crude gesture toward me. I barely even glanced at the empty chair we leave for mother. I started on my food.

Then father decided it was a good time to talk about things I already know. He started by telling me he is "in his death spiral" as if I hadn't already noticed the grey hair on his scalp. Even the most naive royal-blood citizen of Fraun knows what that means. You don't have to be a scholar in the realm of wisdom who studies all nuances and details. Father's hair went grey, therefore he will die inside of the next five annuals. Surely this isn't something he felt the need to tell me.

Then he decided it was necessary to point out another obvious statement. "You will be the next queen of wisdom."

I continued to stare at him, wondering why we were even having this conversation. He continued. "I know you know all this but I'm not sure that you fully grasp what you'll be taking on. I need you to remember that we are tasked with keeping the wisdom and past of Fraun alive. It is our realm that is responsible for overseeing the educational plan of all realms. Without us—" his voice wavered a little here. "Without us, they'd dissolve into baseless fools who argue and use violence. It is our burden to remind them of the reason for civility."

I took this chance to break in and let him know that I already knew all these things. He answered, "There is a difference between knowing something because you've read it in a scroll and experiencing something." He paused here, dramatically running his hands down his face. "Look, I know this doesn't make sense to you yet. But there will come a time after I'm gone when you are ruling things and you won't know what you should do next. There won't be a scroll that can solve it for you, there won't be an obvious answer."

I, quite simply, disagree. There are always scrolls to study and cases to analyze. Surely he's not claiming that something I will go through in my reign will have never had a similar case study? There are always answers if you look deeply enough. Before I could figure out a polite way to disagree with the king of wisdom, he decided he had more to say.

"I need you to remember our realm's purpose. We are the realm of wisdom. We use our brains to guide us, not our hearts. We find the solution that makes the most sense only after analyzing all options. You will not have all the answers all the time, but you are capable of coming up with something that will work. I need you to remember that."

I felt like that moment was becoming entirely too emotional, so I pulled my hand back and tried to show him a brave face. I felt like this was a test and I have always been fantastic at passing tests. So I sat up straight in my chair, restated the question he was asking to buy myself a little time, and then agreed. It sounded something like this.

"You want me to always remember to look through all my options before choosing one? That is common sense. I can promise to do that."

He sighed like he was almost disappointed in me, which is impossible. Then he said, "I want you to remember that there will be things that come up during your rule that have no obvious options. There will be things that stump you."

I don't mean to be rude because King Spec is the ruler of my realm and he deserves respect. But what he is saying is completely false. There have been plenty of rulers before me in my realm and in the others. We have scrolls about all of them. Surely every single one of them has faced something I can draw from. I cannot foresee anything coming my way that is completely unlike everything else. Father is being emotional, not logical. The two often cannot coexist. I will approach any problems that come my way with logic. I will study scrolls from our past to find possible solutions and then I will choose the best one.

However, this is the one concession I will give him. I will start my scroll now and I will write a detailed account myself. Therefore, someday, I will be able to pass this scroll on to the rulers who come after me and they will get a first-hand account. It will not be filtered through another hand or altered at all. Consider this the personal scroll of the future Queen of Wisdom. Learn from her.

20th Annual, 8th Lunar Cycle, Day of the New Moon

The King is dead. He died last night as the last sliver of moon was peeking through clouds in the sky. I called Thometh in to speak with me this morning to tell him. He reacted exactly as expected, with emotions that are not necessary for a situation like this. We are royal blood of Renchenda, we are expected to act with logic at all times. I don't know how else to get through to this child about that. Let me try and explain how our conversation went. I have a good recollection, but some words may have been different.

"The King has passed," I told him.

"Passed? Like he died?" Thometh asked.

"Yes. Today will be the day of grievance for Renchenda. I have alerted the council. Tomorrow, I will be the Queen of Wisdom." I am certain I delivered this message in exactly the tone one should give it. I was direct and clear. I was logical and factual. Emotions and logic often cannot coexist. My brother should learn this now before he is an adult in the eyes of the kingdom.

He, however, chose the opposite reaction. Big tears rolled down his face and he fell to his knees. It was a complete overreaction. "We need to have a funeral for him," he wailed between sobs.

I am sure I rolled my eyes. "We will do no such thing. It is an unnecessary waste of valuable time."

"We should be letting people talk about good memories with Dad. We should be sharing our great times."

"Thometh, you are being overly emotional. We will do no such thing. King Spec is dead. It will not bring him back to share memories. I'm not even sure bringing him back would be wise. Fraunians die, Thometh." I am certain I lowered my voice here, giving him the small comfort of facts delivered quietly and personally. "King Spec knew he would not live forever because none of us do. I will be the best Queen of Wisdom I can be. I will be the comfort Renchenda needs right now."

Thometh stood up again then. He brushed the tears away from his cheeks and rolled his shoulders back. I was hopeful this was a sign that he was ready to be the prince I always wanted him to be. Maybe he would earn a place on the family tree on the wall, which I know father never added him to.

Instead, he disappointed me yet again. He does that a lot.

"I don't like the way you do things," he said.

"You certainly don't have to. Regardless of your emotion, I am the Queen of Wisdom and I will do things in the most logical way. That is the way of our realm."

He shook his head, sending his hair flying. "No, I don't like it. I want to have a funeral for our father and let the citizens of Renchenda grieve."

I sighed, a heavy sound in the otherwise empty room. "That's not going to happen, Thometh. This is not something we are discussing. It is a decision I have already made."

"He was your father," he shouted.

"He was. Now he is dead and I am Queen. This is my decision to make." I stood, smoothing my dress. "We will not discuss this further."

"I'm leaving," he declared suddenly. I admit that wasn't what I was expecting.

"You are only eight annuals. Where would you go? Who would take you in?"

"You don't care. I'd be out of your way and we wouldn't have to deal with each other."

I have to admit, the child had a point. We don't see life the same way. We don't agree on anything. We don't approach problems the same. We have nothing in common at all. I stayed silent, thinking about all of this.

Perhaps Thometh assumed my silence was agreement, which is partially true. Perhaps he just got tired of waiting. More likely, he acted on emotions and just picked his route. Either way, Thometh stormed out of the room and the building at that precise moment.

He didn't come home for dinner. He didn't come home even now, as I am preparing to lie down and get some rest.

I think he may actually have left.

He may have made the first logical decision of his life. Strangely, I'm finally proud of him.

21st Annual, 2nd Lunar Cycle, 4 Suns past Half Moon

I have found a spouse. Top is the son of a respectable merchant in Renchenda. He often helps out at the library in the center of town, keeping inventory of the scrolls and allowing children to check them out. It is a respectable position. I am disappointed that he will be missed in the library, but I am certain we can find someone else for that position. After all, won't he be more effective in caring for the historical scrolls of the royal family?

I always expected that I would marry a spouse that can offer something to Renchenda. I do feel that I have found that match. But something about Top is more than that. When I'm with Top I feel this warmth in my chest that I had only previously heard described by people being overly emotional.

When I started these personal scrolls, I promised to be honest and give a firsthand account of everything I experienced as royalty in Renchenda. Therefore, I need to admit that I believe what I am feeling with Top is love.

This is a concept those of us in Renchenda often have trouble with, for obvious reasons. I cannot explain in words that are adequate what makes me feel this way. I can simply and unhelpfully say only that you will feel it when it happens.

It's like the part of my brain that is always looking for problems and possible solutions is blissfully quiet when I am spending time with Top. My brain is capable of going silent when we are together.

Don't fear, I am also able to work when we are together. Basically, before Top, I was always in work mode. With Top, I can choose whether I am working or relaxing. This is the beauty of love, I believe.

I will be telling Top how I feel today. I expect marriage announcements in the near future. Renchenda will have their King.

22nd Annual, 1st Lunar Cycle, Day Past Quarter Moon

Any day now the Prince or Princess of Renchenda will be gracing us with their presence. The medical tent has taken to sending someone to check on me daily for the last lunar cycle. They report that it will be any day now. My stomach has grown large and cumbersome. I am tired of it being in the way all the time. I am tired of the stretch of my skin. I am ready to be done being pregnant.

Top insists motherhood will be wonderful. He suggests the way I interact with him will be the same as how I interact with the baby. He says the connection will be instantaneous.

I have my doubts. I don't feel warm or connected when the baby moves. I can leave my hand on my stomach and feel what must be a knee or an elbow stretch out and drag under my skin. I don't feel anything when that happens. Sure, it is interesting. But no more so than observing animals beyond our realm in their natural habitat. I am interested in why the baby moves as it does or how it grows there. But I am not invested in the creature it will be to me.

Top is sure that will change.

I am not so sure.

22nd Annual, 1st Lunar Cycle, 2 Suns Past New Moon

This morning the baby arrived.

He is a healthy boy with long legs and arms. He has yellow hair and blue eyes.

The medicine man proclaimed he was healthy immediately. The horns were then blown and the announcement was made across the kingdom. Prince Jordyn of Renchenda is the heir to my throne of wisdom.

Top placed the infant on my chest. I sat with him, holding him and watching him take breaths in and out. Having spoken to many mothers since finding myself pregnant, I know I am expected to feel something now. I believe there was a part of me that hoped Top was right. I hoped to feel the same warmth I feel for my husband, the king, flood my body when I held the little prince. I am almost disappointed that I was right. I feel nothing when I look at the child.

I hold him because I am expected to. I feed him because I know it is illogical to assume he can get necessary nutrients anywhere else.

But I feel nothing.

A woman came to see me. She is from the medicine tent and was tasked with checking on my health and the baby's health. This woman was chatty, telling me all about her own three children. She described an entirely different experience than the one I had. From her, I was able to glean a few important things.

First, this is not a normal reaction when one has given birth. Therefore, it would be beneficial for me to keep my lack of feelings to myself. People may expect me to love my child as I love my husband.

Second, she makes it clear the child will likely feel love for me. This caused me to pause and look at the baby through fresh eyes. Sure, as Queen I am used to being loved by my subjects. But most of them do not have access to me in their daily lives. This child can develop emotions similar to the ones Thometh developed if I am not cautious. Too much access to me might make him illogical, unfocused on the greater good of the Realm.

I cannot let that happen.

I made an important decision after that meeting. I will do my best to be present in the baby's life, helping him to understand the benefit of logical thinking. However, I will not allow him to spend all of his time in my presence.

I informed Top that I wanted to hire a servant or two to help with Prince Jordyn's care. He agreed readily, telling me he wanted me to be able to continue my tasks as Queen.

Top, I noticed, does feel things for the baby. I can see it in the way he smiles at the newborn. I can tell in the way he always wants to be touching him, laying a hand on his head, or brushing the hand. I wonder if Top is better at feeling emotion than I am or if he is simply better at pretending.

23rd Annual, 7th Lunar Cycle, 6 Suns Past Third Quarter Moon

Top and I had an interesting conversation last night. It is one that I have been pondering for well over a lunar cycle, convinced that we had to have it. It's not a conversation I looked forward to having simply because it makes me feel a flood of emotion to even think about his passing. However, I felt it was necessary.

Since Jordyn was born, it has never changed that Top is more connected to the child than I am. I eat breakfast with the child in the morning, making sure that he is receiving the proper diet for a prince of his stature. Then, I complete my work on the third floor of Castle Fraun where I can focus and the noise of the child does not reach me. During the day, he is cared for by two different servants.

I come down for lunch with the child and his servants. Top is normally off at the schools around this time, where he brings scrolls and history lessons to many of the students. After lunch, I will participate in some instruction with Jordyn. The council disagrees with Renchenda's position about the education of smaller Fraunians on this point but in my household, we hold fast to the belief that children are absorbing instruction even when they are not capable of speech.

I read to Jordyn from historical scrolls of the realm

until he begins crying out of some barbaric attempt to communicate discomfort. At this point, the servant will take him and I retire back to the third floor to finish tasks for the day.

Top is home by sunset and we all dine together. Then, in the evening, we spend time together in the castle. I enjoy being in Top's company, as always. He will tell me about his day and I will share information about what tasks I was able to accomplish. All the time we are discussing our routine, he insists on being in contact with the Prince. He will bounce him in his lap, swing him around the room, or roll something between them on the floor. Of course, I know these can be stimulating events for the child, helping him to learn skills he will need in life, but I can think of more beneficial ones.

I can only conclude that my husband does these things with my child merely because they are fun and not because they will help him be a better future King of Wisdom. This conclusion leads me to the next logical one which is that my husband enjoys the presence of my child.

So, the conversation I have been plotting and planning for a lunar cycle went something like this.

"I do not feel as connected to our child as you do."

Top looked tired. Not surprised, which is what I had been expecting, but tired. This told me he had noticed the lack of connection between us as well. Then he responded. "You have to spend time with him, Aine. He will be speaking soon. He will have opinions. Surely you'll be interested in those."

"The ladies from the realm tell me I should feel that connection already like I feel it with you. I am not a good mother, Top. I feel as if you should be aware of this."

"I am aware you feel that way. It will change. He's a good boy and you are a loving person. It is in there, your ability to love."

"It's not logical to assume that I will love a being just because it came from my body," I insisted.

"It is not logical that you would fall in love with me either, but you did."

"I cannot argue with that," I admitted.

In the interest of keeping thorough records, I should admit that at this point the king kissed me and whispered that he loved me. Then he assured me that Jordyn and I would grow to love each other. We were too much alike, he argued, to spend our lives not getting along.

"There's one more thing I want you to be aware of," I said. "Part of being the Queen of Wisdom is understanding my strengths, weaknesses, and limitations. I do not think I am infallible. I understand that I am not." This is part of the speech I had practiced multiple times. I am certain that I said all these words exactly like this. "I need you to understand that if something were ever to happen to you, I would be incapable of raising that child on my own."

Top shook his head and kissed me on the forehead. "You are stronger than you think, Aine. The servants would help you and you would do a fine job of being his sole parent. Relax, I'm not going anywhere."

I am afraid he didn't grasp the magnitude of what I was telling him. He cannot guarantee that he will not die before me. If I die, the Prince becomes the King and will need the support of his common-born father. If he dies, I do not know what happens, but I know I am incapable of raising that child alone. I am positive of that.

24th Annual, 4th Lunar Cycle, Day of Full Moon

My husband is experimenting on me to prove that he was right about my maternal instincts. He's been doing it for lunar cycles now. He has been leaving for periods to conduct business in the realm, leaving me alone with Prince Jordyn. The servants who work in our home do not spend the night. This means if Top is not home for or after dinner time, it is up to me to get the child bathed and into his bed. Of course, I am capable of this. The child is small and has no words yet so there is nothing to prevent me from being able to get this done quickly.

But, I think, Top was hopeful that I would feel some sort of emotional connection to the child during this time. I'm not sure what he thinks would be an appropriate emotion. All I know is that I feel nothing. The child is slippery when the water is coursing off his body, so I have to hold him tighter to keep from dropping him. However, nothing happens in my heart or stomach when I do this. I don't feel safe or important to this child. I am merely a caregiver, like everyone else he comes into contact with during the day. I am starting to realize that not only do I not feel an emotional response to him, but I am also not sure he feels one toward me.

Last night, again, Top had taken to conducting business, and Jordyn and I were alone. I fed him dinner myself. He ate quite a bit more than he normally does which tells me that he is going through a growth spurt. He's already quite a bit larger than the other infants I have seen in the past. His limbs are long and skinny. He will likely be tall. Since height is something we value here, that should make me proud. But serving as further proof that I am not at all maternal, I feel nothing with that realization.

After dinner, I dropped the child into a warm water bath using water from the river that had been warmed over the fire. He seems to enjoy the water, splashing and playing around immediately. I had to give him a stern warning to focus on our task while I was washing him to avoid being splashed. He did comply, which is more than I could ever say for that brother of mine.

The bath concluded with a towel off and some dry clothes. Then, having nothing else I could imagine getting done with a small baby near me, I simply put him in his bed and shut his bedroom door. He did cry for a bit, which is not uncommon, but eventually, he lulled himself to sleep.

When I retired to the third floor to attempt to get a policy scroll updated in front of my warm fire, I found myself unusually sleepy. My eyelids were dropping and I had trouble concentrating. I ended up taking myself to bed early, without getting my work done, to avoid falling asleep at my table. I was incredibly frustrated with this outcome. How can a Queen expect to be the best for her realm if caring for another life makes her too tired to work? This is simply unacceptable.

So, when I received word this morning that Top was not expected home tonight, I asked the servant to stay for the evening. I offered to compensate her with food to take home to her family in the morning from our kitchen. She heartily agreed and spent the day with Jordyn.

I've managed to get the policy scroll updated, a letter sent off to the council, and ruled on eight different letters that have arrived from Renchenda citizens. It has been a productive day!

Just now I went down to the kitchen to get myself some food. I happened upon the servant giving the baby his bath. I noticed she was not discouraging him from splashing and playing, but instead cooing at him which made him laugh a little. I also overheard her tell him in a singsong voice that is not at all her normal voice that his parents were "on vacation".

I am in no such place. I could have popped into the

room to straighten out the error, it is a path I considered. However, that path would have ended with me being in the room with a child who cannot speak and likely didn't understand what she was saying anyway. It would have made her and I feel awkward. It was an emotional response to what I can only assume was jealousy at seeing the prince bonding with someone in a way that he and I are not capable of.

Instead, I went to the kitchen and took a few slices of strawberry before retreating to the attic to eat them.

I have decided Jordyn and I will never have a comfortable relationship. However, I can admit that I am glad he has that with someone. Perhaps it will make him a little more capable of connecting with people than I am.

Perhaps he will be more balanced than I.

24th Annual, 4th Lunar Cycle, 5 Suns past Full Moon

The problem with emotions is that they are impossible to control. Once you allow yourself to feel them, you can no longer stop them. If you allow yourself, for example, to feel love for another person you will also be letting in pain and heartache when you disappoint them or let them down. This is a lesson I am learning the hard way tonight.

Let me explain.

Top came home yesterday earlier than he had expected. When he sent me word that he would be gone again tonight, I had the servant stay. This is proving to be a wonderful solution. I get my work done and Jordyn gets his time with someone he connects with.

Top does not see it that way.

When he found the servant with the baby and me in the upstairs room, he was irate. "You have to get down there and spend time with him. This is why I've been leaving him with you. It's your chance to get to know him and bond. Have you been hiding up here every time I'm gone?"

"Of course," I had answered. The initial anger, I remember, was shocking. I was surprised but pleased to see him at the door. I wanted to embrace him, welcome him home. That was at odds with this angry visage greeting me. I was confused.

He shook his head looking suddenly disappointed in me. "Aine, you aren't even trying. I have never seen you refuse to try something before. What is going on?"

This is when I learned that once you let emotions in, you lose the ability to control them. For the rest of my life to this point, I had been able to avoid all situations where emotions are the default. Letting Top into my heart has broken me. It seems to only have broken me when he is involved. But suddenly, with him in front of me, I felt all kinds of things. Pain, anguish, and failure. I burst into tears, hot and unfamiliar. "I don't know how to be his mother," I sobbed.

Luckily, my husband understands that I am new to these sorts of emotions. He crossed the room, all traces of his anger gone from his face, and embraced me. I was surprised by how much better his strong hands tracing up and down my spine made me feel. I put my head on his shoulder and let him comfort me. "You have to try," he whispered. "Jordyn is an extension of me and you love me, right?"

"Of course I do. You know I do."

"Good. Jordyn is my child too. There is a part of me in there. Find that part of me in the child and hold on to that. You are capable of loving him, I'm sure of it." He pulled back from me then, so he could look me in the eyes. "Aine, I'm six annuals older than you. We both know what that means. I will not live forever. There will come a day when you have to finish raising Jordyn on your own. I need you to be able to find that part of me that is inside of him. I need you to be able to love him as you love me."

"I don't want to think of this," I told him. "You are the best part of me. I don't know who I am without you anymore." I hated admitting this to him, but it is true. It's something I've been reflecting on lately. In my letters to the community when they request things, I find myself thinking of Top and how he would respond. I know my logical side can be too harsh sometimes. Top's emotion has taught me to temper those responses and control how harsh I am. Top is the reason I am the Queen they adore.

He kissed me then. "I know you don't, but you need to. Think about it, since thinking is what you do best."

He is not wrong. I will need to dedicate more time to thinking about what will happen to my realm when Top is no longer with us. I must come up with an acceptable solution. Right now, I'm not seeing those paths.

34th Annual, 7th Lunar Cycle, 1 Sun past Quarter Moon

A quarter of a lunar cycle past my husband awoke with grey hair. This is typical in Fraun and I am embarrassed to admit that it made me upset. I should have understood this was coming. I should have prepared myself for it. I tried to tell myself that I have spent the last ten annuals doing exactly that, preparing for the day when Top leaves me and I have to figure out how to rule Renchenda without him by my side. But when I saw that grey hair on the top of his head, when I knew that he had only five annuals left, at most, before he was gone, I panicked.

I can admit here, where I have pledged to be honest, that I am avoiding him now. I have taken to spending more time up here on the third floor. I am challenging myself to make these ruling decisions completely on my own. How will I react when I cannot talk to him about it? A few of the nights have found me alone up here, still agonizing over a few scrolls for citizens. I find it takes me a lot longer to analyze paths when I cannot allow myself to consult others for possible solutions. I cannot push aside one tricky scroll and return to it over dinner with my husband. Instead, I must force myself to come up with the perfect solution completely on my own

I know that it is evening now. The sun has set, forcing me to light candles and torches in here to continue working. Yet I continued to pore over one problematic scroll from the local school.

Top came to the door of the room, knocking. "Aine, you need to come downstairs for dinner. Jordyn and I would like to spend some time with you."

I tried calling through the door that I was busy, which was the truth. Top was insistent. "Jordyn learned some interesting things from his tutor today. I'm sure he'd like the opportunity to tell you about them." His knocking grew louder and his voice took on a dangerous edge.

I went to the door then because the noise was keeping me from focusing. I opened it just enough to put my face out, holding my foot behind it to prevent Top from opening it more. If he came into that room he might see the scroll. If he saw the scroll, he may offer his advice. I needed to find this solution on my own, without Top's interjections. As much as I value what he brings to the table, he won't always be there to help me. This was again forefront of my mind because the sight of him with a full grey head of hair was right there before me. "I'm trying to finish up a few scrolls. I will join you if I have time," I told him.

"Come to dinner. Then, after Jordyn has gone to bed, we can come back up here and I will help with the scrolls," he offered. "Just as we have done before."

I shook my head. "I cannot do that. You will not be alive forever and I must learn to help these citizens without your assistance."

"Don't be morbid," he accused.

That felt like a physical slap. I wasn't being morbid. I didn't want to think about his death. Death was merely a certainty of life and I was being prepared. It is what we do here in Renchenda, we think about the logical thing and we prepare for it. I have let myself get too attached to Top and his advice. I knew he would not live forever and I have not fully prepared myself to go back to living without him. I hate how much I have let myself rely on him. I intend to force myself to fix this. "I'm being logical," I corrected him.

Top reached out then and brushed his fingers across the side of my face. Odd, although I am past the age where his touch should make me feel like my entire body is on fire, I can still feel that lingering heat. My eyes slip closed for a few heartbeats. "You are brilliant and capable of leading this realm," Top whispered. "You are the best Queen Renchenda has ever seen. Trust yourself." I opened my eyes to find him smiling lovingly at me and felt the urge to throw the door open the rest of the way and run into his arms.

Instead, I reminded myself that this same want

would exist in five annuals but my husband would not be here to quench it. Reminding myself of this gave me the strength for what I said next. "I appreciate your assessment of my abilities, but this is something I must do myself." I shut the door before I could change my mind.

"Aine," Top banged on the door. "This is not the answer, Aine. Your son is downstairs right now, waiting for his dinner. Come down and eat with us."

"You best get down there to eat with him," I replied as calmly as I could. "It's not right to make a boy of only twelve annuals eat by himself."

I know I am making the right choice, making Top's inevitable death easier on me in this way. But hearing his footsteps walking away just now made me have doubts. I had to remind myself that the best path is not always the easiest one.

I'm sure he understands.

36th Annual, 2nd Lunar Cycle, 4 Suns past Full Moon

Jordyn has begun to ask questions about his future rule of the realm. Top seems to think this is reason enough to bring the child to the door of the third floor, disturbing me in my work. "I think you can answer his questions and maybe even get a little input on those scrolls," Top said through the wood.

Over the annuals since his hair has gone grey, Top has tried many things to get me to open that door and let him back into my life. I want to most of the time. I have let him through a few times, opening my heart and my arms to him.

But this was the first time he had said something that truly made logical, not just emotional, sense. Someday when Top is gone, I will have to rule alone. But, someday beyond that, I will also be gone and the child will have to rule the realm.

I opened the door and let Top usher in the small yellow-haired boy with the curious eyes and the awkward limbs of a very tall, almost fully grown Fraunian. Jordyn dropped into an open chair by the fire and his eyes immediately darted to the pile of scrolls. "What are you doing with all of these?" he asked.

"They are requests from citizens, which are a major part of my job."

"Do all the royal people have to answer scrolls like this?" he asked.

I dropped into the chair beside him. "No. Some choose to have the citizens come before them to present their cases. But in Renchenda, we teach all citizens to write and this is a way for them to practice the art of communicating in that form."

He frowned at me, which was an odd expression on his little face. "I think every realm should teach writing."

"It's not something the other royals believe is important. For example, in Sarcheda they value strength.

They don't see a reason to also know writing."

Jordyn's eyes tracked up to the ceiling as he considered this. "Can't they say it's a strength of mind?"

I smiled at the youthful idea. Then I remembered that the boy prince was almost an adult by Fraunian standards and entirely too young to be asking questions like this that he should already know the answer to. "Who is your tutor right now?" I asked, suddenly concerned.

"Fesh, why?"

"It seems like you would understand the simple nature of the realms and their strengths. Sarcheda has no desire to cultivate the strength of the mind, which is our territory. Surely you are aware of that."

Jordyn again tracked his eyes up to the ceiling. This time, he left them there while he spoke. "Just because it is the way it is always done doesn't mean it's the way it always must be."

I must admit, I did like the sound of that. I waited for a beat to see if the child would have anything else to contribute to the conversation, then I pulled the top scroll into my lap and carefully read it again. A citizen was requesting an addition to their residence. They clearly stated the size of the current home, the reason for the addition, and the adequate space available on their lot. This, in my opinion, was an easy solution. I cleared my throat and read it aloud to Jordyn. "What would be the response?" I asked.

Jordyn nodded. "We should allow them to build the addition since there is space and a good reason," he answered.

"I agree," I said, reaching for my feather and ink.

"Of course you agree," the boy continued. "It is policy."

Now, I treated him to a smile. Perhaps he was learning things after all. "Correct."

He watched me as I wrote a response and rerolled the scroll. When I leaned forward to reach for the wax and the seal, I found they were already in Jordyn's hands. He held them out to me one at a time and watched as I used them. Then he took them back, carefully placing them in their exact positions on the table between us.

"Can I ask you about the new King?" Jordyn asked.

King Tin had taken the throne in Sarcheda merely a fortnight ago. He wasn't much older than Jordyn is now and the circumstances by which he came to be King are unusual, at best. I nodded. "If you must."

"I talked to him a little when he was here for the ceremony," Jordyn admitted. "He's young, only sixteen annuals. He has a strong personality and a commanding presence. I guess I just wondered how he's been doing at council meetings. Is he accepted there? Do they have a problem with his age? Is he confrontational?"

I hold up my hand to stop the boy from peppering me with further questions. "You must stop your curiosity from running away with your tongue, child. No one can answer all those questions at once. Slow down and try to prioritize."

"Father says curiosity is a sign of a healthy mind."

I sighed. "He may not be wrong about that but you need to learn to put the most important question first and then wait. At least in that way if a person grows weary of answering your tiresome questions you will have the answer you seek. Try again." I waited him out, watching as his eyes tracked to and from the ceiling pondering and weighing which question was most important.

"Will you allow me to ask more than one question?" he asked cautiously.

"You best hope so because that was already one question."

He closed his eyes tightly and frowned. "Alright, the most important question I have to ask you about that King is this one." His eyes popped open. "Do you think the story about his parents falling to their deaths is entirely a true story?"

It was at this moment that I realized I may have misjudged the intelligence of the prince. Having only met the young King one time he had already picked up on the nuances that led many on the council to suspect foul play at work in Sarcheda. "That is a very good question and one I fear we will never have the answer to. King Tin is the head of that council as King of the first realm. The council does not believe there is a reason to look further into it than they already have. They trust the word of the kings until there is a reason not to."

For a heartbeat, I thought that would be the end of the discussion. So I was surprised when Jordyn spoke again. "I don't think I believe him."

I nodded at him. "I don't think the council cares if the story is true or not. They have their seated kings, things can continue the way they always have."

I realized after I said this, that they will feel the same way about my death when this child becomes the next King of Renchenda.

39th Annual, 7th Lunar Cycle, New Moon

I do not have words to explain the illogical feelings in my body at this moment. I feel it is only important to record this. Top has died.

39th Annual, 7th Lunar Cycle, 3 Suns past New Moon

The child is pounding on the door to the third-floor office. He has been pounding on the door for a long time. I cannot bring myself to answer him. I have tried. I have tried to see the child as a part of Top, as my husband and my love told me to. But I cannot. The child is not just a piece of Top. He is also the worst part of me. He is the logical, incapable of love, balanced with the terrifyingly illogical who will fall with his whole heart someday. Then, when his love dies, he will become like I am now. The logical side of me is at war with the side that has loved. It does not make sense for me to feel this much pain. It does not make sense and I cannot stand things that don't make sense. The child will be this way someday and I cannot bring myself to open that door and allow him to attach to me. I cannot bring myself to be the person he aches for.

39th Annual, 7th Lunar Cycle, 5 Suns past New Moon

He has stopped his insistent banging, thankfully. But the child has not left. I suppose I know better than to call him a child at this point. He is seventeen annuals, an adult in the eyes of the council. Top has spent years bragging to me about how smart he is and how quick he is. He is not a child.

But this behavior, sitting outside in the hallway and refusing to move, is childish. The servants have been bringing him food, I hear them. He eats but he won't leave. I prop myself on the other side of the door, sitting on the floor in my finest clothes. I should eat more than the fruit I have been picking at for many suns, but I cannot bring myself to open the door and allow food to enter. I am sure Jordyn would come with it and bring his pain. I have enough pain on this side of the door, I do not need to allow more to enter.

"He told me this would happen, you know," Jordyn says quietly. I hear the voice of a man float through the wood and it makes me snap my head up to listen. He has his father's voice. Perhaps that is something I can latch onto? "He told me that you would break when he died. He said I needed to try and reach out to you, to give you something to lean on. He said you would feel emotions you could not understand or explain and someone would need to be here for you. But you're not letting me do that. I don't understand why you won't let me do that."

I cannot answer him. Again, I am struck by how right he is and how smart my husband must have been. He knew, even more than I did, how I would react. But why would he send this boy to stand for me? I cannot lean on this boy. I will not.

"I'm hurting too, you know," Jordyn continues. "I relied on him for a lot of my day and he explained a lot of things to me about growing up. He didn't explain how to get through this though, not really. I was hoping we could figure that part out together, you and I. Won't you open the door and let us try?"

I cannot lean on this boy. I cannot.

Honestly, I'm not even sure I want to stand up right now.

Maybe I want to lie down beside Top and let this smart boy Top has raised, the one with Top's voice, lead the realm. Perhaps it is time for that.

The following parchment was found beside the body of Queen Aine of Renchenda on the day of the Quarter Moon following her

39th annual. The medical tent found traces of poisonous leaves in her body. No one is sure when she acquired them or when, exactly, she ingested them. The council concluded this death would have been a suicide, as no one else had been inside the third-floor room of Castle Fraun with her since the death of King Top.

For Jordyn, King of Renchenda,
I am sorry I was never the mother you deserved.
Top was the best father for you. Perhaps the best thing I ever did for you was pick the right man to be your father and role model.
I know rulers of Renchenda should lead with their brains and never their hearts. The moment I fell in love with Top, I had too much heart for the job. I couldn't possibly let you in there as well and make myself a worse Queen. I understand that you were trying to connect with me, but I hope you understand why I could not allow that. There was already too much of me invested in Top. I couldn't spread myself thinner.
I hope that you will take this position and be better than I ever was. Lead with your brain, never your heart. Keep yourself sharp and logical at all times. Be curious, but choose your questions wisely. Don't be sidelined by love, it causes too much pain. Stay focused. Remember the father who raised you, but be better than us both.
I am sorry we couldn't have had it differently but you are who you are anyway. Make the best of it.
Aine

A Changed Man

The door to the grocery store has never properly closed so when Lance leans on it, it pops open. Everyone shopping inside the store pauses what they're doing to turn in his direction. The grocery owner, a squat man who helps get the vegetables from the nearby farm and into these displays, smiles. "Lance, how are the boys?" He greets.

"Getting older every day," Lance brags. "Lawrence is seventeen annuals now and Esteban is finally fifteen. Their hair is a good length now that it has stopped growing. I'm living in a home with two men."

The grocer laughs. "What are they planning to do with their lives? How will they help Enchenda grow?"

"We're working on that." Lance feels a sense of pride in his sons. One that can only come from knowing you have raised good men. They were top of their classes at school, both are strong in the garden, and they are the kind of caring individuals his chosen realm requires. The youngest son, Bin, is only five annuals and barely capable of speech.   But these men who he has raised make him proud every single day.

Lance moves around the market, selecting produce and interacting with a few of the Fraunians. Many ask about his sons and a few ask about his wife. It's clear that these are the best parts of him. Without his family, what would people talk to him about? What would he have to offer Enchenda outside of a pair of well-taught and well-mannered men? He knows his family is his legacy.

Back at home, Lance calls out his arrival and drops the produce on the counter. He leans in to kiss Becca on the cheek. "How are you this morning?" he asks.

"I am perfect. Bin is bumbling through sentences like he knows he is five annuals behind in telling all the stories he's thought up since he was born. The others are off hunting, they should be back soon."

Lance slips a tomato from the pile on the counter and reaches for a sharp knife. "Have you talked to the boys about what they want to do now that they are considered adults?"

Becca, elbows deep in some warm water, sighs. "I tried. Lawrence keeps saying he wants to see the world, whatever that means. Now that Esteban is of age, he seems to be bent on joining him to do the same.”

“Our world is Enchenda,” Lance says, his voice a little too loud for the room. “But I know you know that.” He sighs, the sound evidence of the repetition of this same conversation with no resolution. “Maybe we should just let them see for themselves.”

Becca pulls her hands out of the water, sloshing some down the front of her dress. The light gray fabric turns dark, spreading out along her front like clouds coming before a storm. “Excuse me?”

Lance puts the knife back down on the counter with a clatter and turns to his wife. “We have been having this argument for two annuals. Lawrence has listened out of respect for us, but he’s not happy here. He wants to see what else is out there. Fraun is made up of four other realms. Maybe we should let him explore some of those realms. What would be so bad about having a son who decides to reside over the border in Farcheda? We could still visit.” Lance can see Becca’s anger breaking apart. He takes a step toward her and pulls her into the circle of his arms. He hugs her tight, resting his chin on her head. “I want the boys to be safe and happy. If that means I have to let them see the rest of Fraun, then I think I can do that.”

“Would they be safe?” she mumbles into his chest.

“How could they not be?” Lance pulls back from her so he can see her beautiful face. “What in Fraun can hurt anyone? We’re the safest kingdom there is.”

Lance opens the door as the sunlight is fading and bellows out into the yard "Your mother is putting dinner on the table." Lawrence and Esteban are both there, chopping wood and laughing about something. They look up and wave to him in acknowledgment. He lets the door to the home shut and makes his way to the kitchen to help carry a bowl of food to the table. Becca has prepared a meat dish, ant by the smell, and a vegetable dish that looks like it is mostly tomato. "This smells wonderful," Lance tells her.

"It's basic," she answers.

"Basic is my favorite." Lance winks at her and she smiles. "I don't need anything beyond basic," he adds. As he reaches over Bin's head to place the bowl on the table. He caresses the youngest boy's hair. "One healthy family and enough food to keep us all healthy is the best I can ask for."

They each take a chair at about the same time the two grown boys open the front door. There are empty chairs at the table on each side of Bin, waiting for his brothers to fill them. "Wash your hands," Becca scolds, tipping her head toward the bucket of water she used for washing up some of the dinner things. Her eldest sons head immediately to it, submerging their dirty hands in cold water and scrubbing loose the particles of dirt. Lance watches them out of the corner of his eye even though the days of having to tell them to scrub harder, use the herbs, or dry their hands when they are done are long gone. These are no longer young boys standing in his kitchen. The reminder will help him get through the planned dinner conversation.

Once they take their seats and everyone has a plate of food, Lance wastes no time getting to the point. "You two are going to need to choose what you will do for your future. The town is already asking about it. Let's be honest with each other, tell your mother and me what you have decided."

"If you haven't decided, tell us what you're thinking," Becca adds. "Perhaps we can be of some assistance."

The two boys exchange a look over the top of their youngest brother's head. Lance doesn't miss it. They've definitely talked about this already. "We sort of think maybe we will try something a little different," Esteban says. His voice is quiet and he's looking down at the table instead of at anyone in the family.

Lance takes a deep breath. "Go on," he says. He has to try and keep himself calm. Clearly, the boys are expecting him to be upset by this decision, whatever it is. What he told Becca is true, he's expecting the boys to tell him they want to try living in some other realm. He can handle that. Farcheda and Sarcheda are the next realms over, each sharing a border with either side of Enchenda

Even Renchenda and Marchenda are not far if you travel by animal. They can make this work. He reaches under the table and squeezes Becca's hand for support. She squeezes right back.

"We don't think we'll stay in Enchenda," Lawrence says.

"Where are you thinking of putting up residence?" Lance asks.

"We want to join the Scouts," Esteban answers.

For a moment, Lance cannot move. He's aware of his beating heart, aware of his breath coming and going, but the rest of him has ceased to exist. He feels Becca squeeze his hand again, trying to remind him to stay calm. He blinks a few times and focuses on the faces of his boys, the boys he has tried to keep safe within Fraun's borders since the day they were born. His eyes fill with tears. "You want to do what?" he asks. He heard them, but for some reason, he is hoping they'll say something different.

"C'mon, Dad, don't be difficult," Lawrence chides. "We want to join the Scouts. I was talking to a couple of guys at the fields and the Scouts give you a chance to travel. Did you know they visit things left behind by the giants? They travel there on foot, get things that would be helpful to Fraun, and send them back. It's amazing. I'd be the first Fraunian to have my hands on something that hasn't been touched since a giant. Isn't that epic?"

"We'd be the first," Esteban corrects. "Plus they get

some weapons training for safety." He looks up at his mother, his eyes flashing with excitement. "In case we encounter animals or anything, we'd be taught how to either get away from it or how to kill it so we can have meat to eat."

"So you'd be safe?" Becca asks.

"We'd be surrounded by other people who are experts in safety, Ma. We'd be safe," Lawrence assures her. "We don't even have to do this forever, we just want to give it a try. Maybe a couple of annuals. Then we can come back here and get some boring job at the grocer or something."

It doesn't escape Lance's brain that both boys are truly excited about this idea. It's not one making the plans and the other blindly following, they both have aspects they're looking forward to. It doesn't sound like they've fully thought out everything that will be involved or have a full plan, but they've started and he's proud of them for that. He smiles across the table at them both. "That sounds like a good start," he tells them. "You let us know what we can do to help you make that happen. "

Under the table, Becca slips her hand from his.

Lance can tell from the silence continuing to radiate from Becca after the kids have all turned in for the night that she truly is upset at the way he handled the announcement from their oldest children. He walks up behind her, laying his hand on her hip. "I can make that for you," he offers, obviously talking about the cup of tea she was brewing for herself.

Becca sighs and steps away from the counter. She moves across the kitchen and crosses her arms over her chest, glaring at him. Lance resumes what she had been doing, carefully pulling the leaves off the stems and setting them in the steeping cloth. "Why don't you tell me why you're upset," he offers.

"I'm not upset," she says. But her voice is clipped, angry.

Lance wants to roll his eyes at the obvious lie but can't risk her seeing the motion. Instead, he reaches for the container of dried chamomile heads and selects one to drop into the steeping cloth. "Do you want mint?" he asks, risking a glance over his shoulder.

"No." Becca sighs again, the sound loud and dramatic in the otherwise quiet house. "We can tell them they're not allowed to go. They can take jobs here, helping Enchenda. Or they can travel to the rest of Fraun as you told me they were going to do. But they'll stay safe."

Lance wraps the steeping cloth closed and ties it with a small length of string. Then he drops it into a mug and ladles in some boiling water. The smell wafts up to his nose as he buoys the bag in the steaming liquid. He turns, offering her the cup. "They would be angry and resentful.

Then, because they're adults, they'd likely do it anyway. This way we can agree to work with them and help them make plans that are the safest way to go about this work."

"The life of a Scout is dangerous," Becca says. But she takes the mug, which Lance supposes is proof that she's not really mad at him.

"Life, in general, is dangerous," Lance says. Becca pulls the cup away from her mouth and narrows her eyes at him. He rushes to continue. "That boy from down the street died of a stomach ache when he was only twelve annuals, Marty was carried off by a bird as a full grown adult, Kings and Queens have fallen down the ravine, tree trimmers and nest removers have fallen out of trees …" he's ready to continue the list but Becca waves her hand, conceding the point. "Accidents can happen anywhere. We've taught the boys to be smart and resourceful, this is what they want to do."

Becca turns what was likely to be another sigh into blowing onto her tea before taking a big sip. Lance watches her and knows, deep down, that she will agree with him. They're good for each other because they agree on the big things. One of those big things was always raising their boys to be independent and intelligent. They cannot be angry that their eldest two have taken that and run with it, no matter how dangerous it might be. When she turns her eyes to him, they are full of water but her smile appears anyway. "We can help them make plans to do it safely," she says.

"As safely as possible," Lance agrees. "We can make sure they write us letters."

"I'm sure they plan to."

Becca sniffs. "Fine. We'll do it their way." She takes another sip of her tea and Lance closes the last of the space between them, wrapping his arms around her waist and kissing the top of her head.

"I love you," he tells her.

"I know. I love you, too."

"They'll be safe. The Scouts are out in the wild but they're well-trained. The boys are smart. You'll see, it'll work out. I have a good feeling."

"What is that noise?" Becca's voice pulls Lance from sleep the next morning. Morning isn't the right word, he realizes. The sun isn't yet coming through the window beside him. Now that he's awake he hears what woke her. A sound is coming from outside. He stands and pushes the fabric on the window aside, peering into the front yard.

The sun is rising, sending small rays of light around. Enough light that Lance can see the four grown men standing on his lawn wearing muted and dark colors he hasn't seen much of. Fraunians around here tend to wear a lot of shades of green, the color of Enchenda. These men are wearing mostly browns. "I think it's Scouts," he tells

Becca.

"That was quick. The boys only said they wanted to join up one sun ago. They are already here?" She sits up, pulling the covers up with her. "Lance, how much time do we have?"

"I'm not sure. Let me find out." He crosses the room and grabs himself a jacket. The air outside is crisp and he can see his breath puff out in front of him. "Good morning," he calls to the men. "Can I help you lot with something?"

"They're here for us, Dad," Lawrence says as he steps out of the front door. "We have training today."

Lance steps off to the side, letting both of his boys slide past him. The tallest of the Scouts kicks a piece of wood on the ground beside him. "We'll start with simple tools and progress up to things with sharp edges. You have a lot to learn."

Without argument, his two boys follow the directions of the Scouts. Lance watches them practice a balanced stance, learn how to move their arms, and even what animals to watch out for.

Becca comes out at one point, bringing water for everyone in the group. There is a part of Lance that knows he should leave, head back inside and let his boys learn this material on their own. But there is another, larger, part of him that can't do that. This is the part of him that was awakened the day he was handed Lawrence's tiny body for the first time. The part of him that instinctively knows what to do when one of the boys gets a fever or is vomiting. So he sits on his front lawn and watches as a group of men teach his boys skills they may need to survive.

When they finally take a break, Lance sees his chance to get more information. He rises and approaches the Scouts. "I'm Lance," he offers. "It's a nice thing you all are doing, getting the boys ready."

"I see no boys out here," the tall one says. "These two are men."

"Right. Sometimes it's hard not to see them as children. Do you have children?" Lance asks.

"None of my own, no." He offers his hand. "I'm Kristoff. This here is part of my troop."

They shake hands. "They'll be joining your troop then?" Lance asks. "How many are you? Where do you make camp?"

Kristoff nods. "They can join me. These are good men here, we can do with good strong men. We have eight total in our troop, including me. We make camp all over, of course, but mostly we are in the woods just here beyond this land."

"What is the biggest danger in your line of work?" He finds himself curious, not only for his sons but also in general. He has watched these men deliver training that would help with harvesting as well as animals. What must a day be like for these men?

"Animals," Kristoff answers. "They're unpredictable and don't like being disturbed when they've had the run of a particular area. If we crash into their home turf unannounced things can get a little dicey. We try not to harm anything, but we'll defend our troop if we must."

"Do you eat what you kill, then?"

"Absolutely. We leave nothing to waste. Isn't it the same here in Fraun?"

Lance nods quickly. It is the Fraunian way to eat every part of an animal that was killed to provide you with food. Fraunians will put animals' bones and hides to use in buildings or clothing, making sure nothing that is useful is wasted. He's glad to hear that his boys can continue this in the Scouts.

A younger Scout seated on the ground beside Kristoff yawns. "You worried about them dying?" the boy asks on the back of his yawn.

Lance smiles at the direct question. "A father always worries."

"I wouldn't know about that," the kid says, readjusting his legs underneath him. "I ain't got one of those and I sure ain't one myself." He gives up on getting comfortable, instead pushing himself to stand. Lance wonders if he is full height, his head barely reaching to Lance's shoulder. "Kristoff is the closest I got. We'll take care of them like they was family if they join us. That's our way."

Lance nods, appreciating the sentiment.

Kristoff waves his hands. "Alright, we're heading out. We'll be back at sunrise tomorrow to collect you. Bring only what you can carry on your back." He reaches out and pats both Lawrence and Esteban on the back. "I'll be judging you on what you think you need in that bag, so choose wisely."

Lance spins, taking in both of his boys who are nodding as if this is exactly what they expected. "Tomorrow?" he asks. "Did he say you were leaving tomorrow?"

Behind him, he's relatively certain at least one of the Scouts is chuckling. "Dad, can we take this inside?" Esteban asks. "Please."

"Did you know you were leaving tomorrow?" he asks, raising his voice. "Did you think to tell your mother?"

Lawrence steps forward, laying his hand on his father's arm. "Dad, let's go inside and talk about this." He lowers his voice. "You're making a scene."

Lance lets himself be led into the house where he has raised these men. Raised them to believe in putting Fraun first. To believe in not wasting. To believe in treating all creatures with kindness and empathy. He sits in a chair at the table he built with his own hands and looks at the two men he raised. "This is the best decision?" he asks, proud of himself for letting his anger dissipate.

"There's no reason to delay," Lawrence explains. "They're heading out with a list from King Gregario, items that he wishes them to bring back if they can find them. They're leaving tomorrow. Esteban and I would like to be of assistance."

"We'll be back," Esteban says. "We'll have to return to Enchenda when we find what the King has asked for. It shouldn't be a long trip. Kristoff thinks maybe a fortnight, at most."

Lance knows they've put thought into this. He should be proud of their decision-making skills, and he is. But he's also terrified. As a parent, he knows it is easier to protect them when he keeps them close. Outside of the boundaries of Fraun, who will keep them safe? Who will watch over them? He hangs his head, knowing that they will have to watch out for each other. "I'll tell your mother," he says. "Take a walk and give me time to do that."

"Thanks, Dad," Esteban says. "You're the best."

"We'll be alright," Lawrence says, his hand on the handle of the door. "We have each other."

It takes Lance at least eight suns to get used to the fact that the boys are not going to be there when he wakes up. Not going to be there when he comes home from the fields. Not going to be there when they sit down to dinner. One night early on, he sets a plate in front of the chairs they used to occupy. When he sees the pained look on Becca's face, he makes a stronger effort to remember not to do that again.

Becca never gets used to the empty house, not during that fortnight. She lets a few tears leak out, worried about her oldest sons. Anything can happen out there. She knows that. But she also knows that her boys are responsible. They're strong. They're together. During the fourteen suns that they are gone for this first trip, she never really relaxes.

The door to the small house flings open just before sunrise on what would be the fifteenth sunrise since the scout troop took the oldest children of the house out for their expedition. "We're home," Esteban's voice calls. "Is anyone awake yet?"

Although they weren't, Lance and Becca's eyes spring open at the welcome sound and the two practically run from the room. Lance grabs Lawrence and Becca Esteban. They hug with everything they can, squeezing to be sure the men are really standing here. Then they switch children, checking the other in the same way.

Finally, they stand back and look both boys up and down. They appear whole, healthy, and happy. "How was it?" Lance asks.

"Amazing," Lawrence answers.

"Do you have anything to eat?" Esteban asks, his attention on his mother, the chef of the house.

"Didn't they feed you on this journey?" she teases.

"We skipped breakfast this morning to come home, we knew you'd be worried."

"I wasn't worried," Becca says. Although she was, it seems silly now when both boys are safely before her as if they never left. "We have tomatoes and cucumber. Should I make you a salad?"

"That sounds grand." Esteban follows her toward the kitchen. "I'll make some tea if you have any leaves."

"You know we do," she says. "Did you drink only water on the journey?"

"Aye, mostly. Water is easier to come by. You can drink it straight off a leaf or from a stream. We didn't often bother with adding leaves to give it flavor."

"But now that you're home you'll gladly take some?" Lance offers.

"You know it," Lawrence agrees.

Lawrence and Lance take seats at the table, close enough to the kitchen to continue to be part of the conversation but out of the way of the breakfast preparations. "We had a grand time," Lawrence begins. "The forest is so thick and dense, you can hardly see the animals although you can hear them in their homes."

Becca pauses, her hands full of vegetables. "Don't worry, Mom," Esteban says, bumping her lightly with his hip. "They're in their own homes and not a bother to us so long as we don't bother them. We didn't have any interactions with animals at all. Promise."

She visibly relaxes and resumes her work.

At the table, Lawrence also continues. "We got to travel out to a massive building. The houses the giants lived in basically look like ours I guess, but they're just larger than you can imagine. We could only really see the whole thing as we were walking up toward it. You can see for quite a distance, there's just no hiding it. Inside it was loaded with things that we could sort of look through. We were able to find the wood King Gregario was looking for easily enough."

"He also wanted food," Esteban adds from the kitchen where he's muddling leaves for tea. "We couldn't get that from the houses the giants once lived in because everything there has either been taken or has spoiled. So we had to get some of it from the forest. There are all sorts of mushrooms and things growing wild. We learned all about which ones are safe and which ones aren't so we won't go eating anything dangerous by accident."

Lance smiles to himself at the excitement pouring from the boys. "There are a lot of people in this group you're traveling with?" he asks.

"A fair amount. Enough to help bring the materials back but not too many to make noise. It was nice, Dad, being able to carry back food and wood that I knew our Realm needed," Lawrence answers. "We made a difference this trip."

Becca brings the salad of cubed tomatoes and cucumbers to the table, setting a large bowl right in the center. "Dig in," she says. Lawrence reaches in and grabs a handful, popping it in his mouth and chewing with obvious ecstasy. "We haven't had access to a fresh garden in a fortnight, Mom. This is great," he says when he has swallowed the bite. "You're the best."

Lance and Becca exchange a pleasant glance as they watch their boys eat every last morsel. It's a look that says all's right with the world because their boys are home.

The third time Lawrence and Esteban pack up their bags to leave with the Scouts, Lance is shocked to find it feels easier to let them go. He stands on the front lawn with Bin's small hand inside his and waves to them. Bin eagerly chirps "goodbye big brothers", proud of himself for having the voice to say things like this. Lance laughs and scoops up the smaller boy. Together they watch the boys until they can't see them anymore and the forest surrounding Enchenda seems to swallow them up. Only then, and only briefly, does Lance feel the lump of nerves in his throat. He bounces Bin a few times and brings him inside the house, focused on the day ahead and what needs to happen to keep his mind occupied while the older ones are gone.

Bin is now in school in the center of town, because of his age. During the day when the house is empty of the children she is raising, Becca spends her time stitching together fabric into clothing for people in town. She will trade these for food, oils, and other things her family needs in the town square. She makes them in various sizes and lengths for all sorts of people in Enchenda. Her mind naturally can recall the sizes that would be needed for her family of five and, from there, she can make adjustments to offer other sizes. Smaller sleeves, maybe, than she would prefer. Or longer legs than any of her boys have. Her mind wanders a bit when she is stitching and it seems to always flutter between the people in her life she has to worry about. She spends time during these moments wondering what the eldest boys are doing out there in the woods, but not nearly as much time as she spent worrying at that point when they left the first time. Lance was right, it gets easier.

Lance spends his time doing odd jobs around Enchenda for his neighbors. Fixing roofs, trimming trees, cutting back weeds, and even catching earthworms for an elderly woman who had lost her husband. Around Enchenda, it's well known that Lance is the Fraunian who tends to the town square and keeps it looking nice. It's not unusual for citizens to ask him to help with their properties or to teach them how to keep them nice. Sometimes, when he is especially busy, he has to pass along the names of other citizens who can help instead. But now, when he needs to keep his mind off the worries niggling in the back of his mind, he takes them all. Even when it often makes him late for dinner.

He's late for dinner on the fourteenth night they've been without Lawrence and Esteban. When he comes in the door, Becca and Bin are already at the table. Bin is in the midst of a story from school involving many hand gestures and wild sounds. Becca is smiling, but it looks forced. She's annoyed with him, surely for being late. He rounds the room and kisses her on the cheek before dropping into the chair left for him. "I'm sorry for being late," he says. "I was helping with loose boards in Murphy's roof. The sky looks dark near Renchenda as if a storm is brewing in that direction. If it comes this way and we get rain I don't want the Murphy's getting wet."

"It had to be done today?" Becca asks, barely looking up from her plate of food.

"I didn't have to be, no. But I wanted it to be. The boys will be home tomorrow and I'd like to spend time here all together. I didn't want her to expect me to do it tomorrow."

She nods but Lance can tell from the tight line of her lips that she is not happy. He looks around and sighs. The empty house, where she is spending much of her time because she works out of the home, feels oppressive when you're alone. This house was built for a large family. It was meant to allow four or five people to move around. When you're alone the space is too much. It's a reminder that you are waiting on the rest of your heart to be safe. He reaches out and squeezes her hand. "I'm sorry, I was thinking only of myself. I'll do better."

She finally looks at him and offers him a squeeze in return. "Try to," she says.

When she drops his hand and turns her attention back to Bin it feels as though the tension in the room has dissipated. Lance digs into the dish in front of him and revels in the company of his youngest child as he raves about the new friends he made at school.

Lance wakes the next morning with an angry pit in the center of his stomach like a swarm of fire ants has taken residence there. He rubs the sleep from his eyes and sits up, looking around the room. For a beat, he cannot place why he might be feeling like this. Then, like freezing rain falling from the sky and soaking his entire body, it comes to him. The sun is up. It is the fifteenth time the sun has come up since Lawrence and Esteban left. They should be home.

Lance doesn't work that day. That may seem ordinary but the truth was obvious in the way no less than ten citizens of Enchenda show up to "check on him". Each of these ten finds him in increasing levels of distress as the sun treks across the sky. Staring into the distance in the morning light becomes awkward attempts at household chores for distraction by midday and angry pacing by the setting sun.

In a strict reversal of their ordinary roles, Becca remains the positive one. Throughout the day she repeats the idea that the Scout excursion simply "took longer than planned" and that the boys will have "extraordinary tales" when they arrive home.

Lance, who has never been on the receiving end of a chipper attitude when your stomach is gripped with a terrible sour feeling, finds it unbearably annoying. He vows to never be that person again. A positive outlook only helps when you possess it, he learns, it isn't something you can verbally share with another.

By the time the hesitant knock on the door comes, which is just after sunset, it turns out only one of the two moods has successfully passed to the other Fraunian in the house. Both Becca and Lance have defeatedly dropped into silent fear and frustration at the kitchen table. Even Bin, who is the only part of the sad trio with dinner in front of him, seems to recognize that something is off in the household. His usual babble about his day is absent. Instead, the house practically hums with a weighted silence.

Lance stands first at the knock, part of him already beginning to quake with fear. After all, the boys wouldn't knock. They never have before. He exchanges a silent look with his wife. One that communicates a warning that he isn't sure he is strong enough for what is coming as well as a promise to try and be for her sake.

When Lance pulls the wooden door open to find Kristoff, the Scout in charge of the troop, he isn't surprised. He is, however, shocked to see obvious tear tracks down the road-weary face. When the older Scout simply shakes his head and mumbles "I'm sorry—" Lance crumbles. As if he knew it was coming, Kristoff catches Lance under the arms and gently brings him to his knees in an embrace.

Lance doesn't hear the rest of the story, told to Becca over his head. He doesn't hear how Esteban encountered a bird and tried to scare it away from the troop. How Lawrence ran toward the scene when the bird carried his younger brother into the sky. How the arrow, meant for the bird, had struck Lawrence. How the troop had tried to save the elder boy and may have done, had the body of the younger brother not been found. He doesn't hear how Lawrence crumbled at what was left of his brother's body. How they'd lain together as Lawrence's heart stopped to match the void that was the beat of Esteban's.

Becca finds small comfort in knowing they'd been together in the end. But she can't stomach the idea of their final moments being so painful. She wants to scream at Lance for talking her into letting them go, but one look at the heap that is her husband tells her he is already suffering enough. She wants to scream at Kristoff for coming back here, alive, to tell her that her boys are gone. But, truly, he looks as though he already regrets it. She has a feeling he would tell her he would exchange places with them if such a thing were possible. Instead, she turns to the only person in the room who needs her to be strong right now. The one who will not understand what is happening. She scoops Bin up in her arms and settles on the floor with him in her lap. Then, in a whisper, she proceeds to explain what has happened.

Those of us adept at Fraun history already know Lance will become the Fraunian who would turn lost Enchenda men into gardeners and handymen, giving them something to live for when they feel as though they have lost it all. We already know he will find it in his heart to forgive the Scouts, fight alongside them, and understand the joy his sons felt in traveling. We know he will reunite with Bin and Becca someday. But that day, with a sadness that felt too big for his small frame, Lance turned his back on the conversation and walked out of the door to his own house and into the forest. No one followed him.

Tin's Tale

Chapter 1

My parents never had any other children. The way my mother tells the story, I was perfect. There was no need to keep trying. This, of course, is only partially true. It's true in my mother's mind, she's made it true after annuals of telling it to herself over and over again. But, in the beginning, it wasn't true.

There were only two truths that mattered on the day that I was born. The first is that I was the legitimate son of King Todd, a direct descendant whose lineage can be traced back to the first King of Fraun, Oberian, through his strongest son, Sarcheda. The second truth is equally important. I was a boy.

In my family history, males were adored. My family

is royal blood in a realm known for strength. Women were considered the weaker sex. For this reason, female babies born to my family had a way of disappearing. I grew up being quizzed on the family tree painted on the wall of my family home. I knew that I was the ninth male born from my direct line since Sarcheda himself. My mother had hinted to me that she was born to an influential family in Sarcheda, but she would not talk about this when the King was around. Her history was not important. Her family didn't give me my royal blood. Her family didn't make me a prince.

"Prince Tin," a voice interrupts my thinking. I turn away from the wall and find my tutor standing in the dark hall, his arms behind his back. Everything about Marcus would normally be measured against me and found lacking. He is eight clicks shorter than me in a society that values height. He is rounder in the gut than I am. Although my hair has not even ceased to grow, I can also lift more than he can. But Marcus has been my tutor for as long as I can remember and something about him commands my respect. It always has.

"Yes," I answer.

"I need you to come with me, Majesty," he says. "The new servant has been hired. He will be in charge of areas of the family home in which you are regularly in. He is expected to accompany you whenever you leave the home."

I puff my chest out. "I don't need protection," I say. The reaction is instinctual. It's foolish, I know. I have not reached adulthood yet in our society. Couple that with the fact that I am the only prince of the realm and you may reach the conclusion that I am in danger. My father has certainly reached that conclusion and I cannot argue with the King. I can, however, make the show of strength that is required to argue with a tutor.

"It is not for safety. I cannot tell you what it is for. I know only that your father wills it, Majesty." Marcus bows his head. "I am sorry it displeases you. The boy has already been hired. I did my best to make sure it was someone I felt you could connect with." Marcus raises his head and I notice a glint of something in his brown eyes. Mischief, perhaps? "I do believe you'll find this young Sarcheda citizen someone who you can manipulate, Prince Tin."

This thought is pleasing, indeed. It brings a smile to my face to imagine having another young boy who wants my life. Convincing this common citizen that I am the perfect prince with the coveted life could be fun. "Take me to him, then I will decide," I answer.

"As you wish." This time, when Marcus bows, it is not only his head that folds. This is a full bow. A respectful bow for the ruler I will be.

I follow Marcus out of the room and down the dark hallway. The torches he guides me past have been lit, meaning he walked this route to get to me today. Our footsteps echo on the stones, but there are no other sounds in the home.

He opens a door and stands to the side to allow me to enter the room first, as is a custom treatment for those of royal blood. There is a young boy in the center of the room. He has black hair but his skin is lighter than my family's. He is young, perhaps not even full height. I take notice of his outfit, red shirt and black pants. They look as though they are too large for him, meaning he likely comes from a family who cannot afford to have the clothing altered properly. He is not wearing shoes, although that is common for Sarcheda citizens in this warmer weather. "How old are you?" I ask, my voice bouncing off the walls of the small room and echoing around us. Before he can answer I hit him with another question, "Are you even old enough to be capable of speech?"

In Fraun, citizens who have reached five annuals are capable of speech. This boy is small and young. Again, I have to wonder about the purpose of his being hired to work around me and accompany me to town. If my father wished me to have safety, wouldn't he have hired a larger boy?

"Nine annuals, Majesty," the boy answers. He bows deep, his nose practically reaching the clean stones of the floor.

I step closer to him, my feet falling heavy and slow. I squint my eyes as I consider him, now standing fully again before me. He waits as I walk around him as I would a roach for consideration, as if he were property of mine. When I am again facing him, I cross my arms. "You are much younger than me. I am fourteen annuals, perhaps you already knew that. You obviously aren't for my protection. Tell me what your new job is, as you see it," I command.

"I am to keep you happy, Majesty."

"How do you plan to do that?" I ask.

"I will keep your home clean, fetch you food and water if you need it, hire you a roach if you require transportation, and speak to any common citizens you wish me to speak to on your behalf."

I like the sound of all this, of course. But I still don't understand why my father wished for this. Behind me, Marcus clears his throat. "Prince Tin, a word," he says.

"Wait here," I tell the boy. Then I turn and walk to Marcus. I stand in the doorway, my back to the new hire.

Marcus leans in so he can speak to me in secret. "Your father has a man he treats in much the same way," Marcus points out. "He has a servant dedicated to his needs and happiness, surely you've noticed this."

"I have," I answer. I prefer not to think about this man too much. My father has been known to delegate everything, including the discipline of his only son, to this man. The thought, which I was trying to avoid, makes me flinch. I hate the show of weakness and I'm grateful my father wasn't here to witness it. I hope Marcus doesn't feel the need to tell his king. "Is that what this boy is to be for me?" I ask.

Marcus takes his time answering. He seems to roll the question around in his mouth, tasting it. He smiles at me like I am dinner being offered to him after a period of fasting. "He could be. Right now I believe he is a peace offering. You and I both know that your mother believed your father was wrong the other night. His punishment was too harsh."

I flinch at the memory of my father's fist, the strongest one in the realm, landing between my shoulder blades and along my side. For a breath, it feels real again. I can almost imagine I'm curled in a ball on the floor, my instinct to protect myself. I can hear my father screaming at me, his anger growing stronger the more I pull back from him. "This is what I'm talking about," he screams in my head. "Look at how weak you are. Why are you turning from this confrontation? Show me strength!"

I clench my teeth, ball my fists, and force the memory out of my head. "What is your point?" I ask.

"I think she suggested your father do something kind for you. This," Marcus gestures behind me to the boy who must still be standing there, waiting for instruction, "is your peace offering. Your father sees this as a gift, a kindness."

"He is young," I say.

"That he is. Young and impressionable."

I turn and look again at the frail, small boy. I imagine him larger, older, full height. I imagine he will have an impressive body structure if he is trained right and fed the proper diet. I approach him again. "You are from Sarcheda, yes?"

"Yes," he answers.

"You have a family? How many of them live in your home?" I know homes in Sarcheda typically hold more than my family home. Three people in one house is unusual, but we are not ordinary. We are royal blood. Besides, we have servants who also live in our home to meet our every need.

"Four others," he answers. "All older than myself."

I nod as if this matters to me, which it doesn't. "Where is your home?" It may sound as though I care about this child. I don't, not really. What I care about is how long it will take him to get to my family home each morning.

"We're on the edge of Sarcheda, sir. Near the ravine." He gestures with his hand, off to the North.

"If there were an empty room at my family home and you were needed, is there anything to prevent you from being allowed to stay here?" I ask.

He doesn't pause, doesn't need to consider it. The answer is automatic, which earns him some of my hard-to-come-by respect. "Nothing would prevent that, Majesty."

"Alright," I nod at him. "I accept your position as

my servant." I decide this is exactly what I will call him when people ask. My father has hired me a servant, I think. I can work with that.

I turn to leave the room. I'm one step from the door when I think to ask him something I probably should have asked when I met him. I turn back toward him. "What is your name?"

He smiles, glad to be asked the question that likely makes him feel as though we are to be friends. This is an important impression to give him if I desire to mold him to my whims. "My name is Toby," he answers. "It's a pleasure to meet you."

Chapter 2

That afternoon I do my best to forget about Toby. I don't want him to think we are close, not yet. I also don't want him to think I have free time in the afternoon that I can spend with him at the drop of a hat. I need to appear busy and important. For this reason, I spend much of the afternoon moving around our family home as if I have some schedule and purpose. In reality, I have nothing I need to do beyond my strength training right before dinner.

As the sun dips down toward the horizon, I snag a nearby servant. "I'm looking for Toby, the new hire. My personal servant," I add.

The woman smiles at me and bows. "He is in your chambers, Majesty. He was told to clean the hearth."

I smile. "Wonderful, thank you." I head to my bedroom, which is the smallest room located the farthest from the front door. Even though it is warm outside today, it is cold in this room. It is always cold in this room. I would like nothing more than to be able to sleep in my father's bedroom, the largest and warmest one in the house. But that is not my role, not now, not yet. Someday I will be the King of Sarcheda and then I will be as unstoppable as my father.

I open the bedroom door and find young Toby on his hands and knees brushing out the ashes from my hearth. "How has your afternoon been?" I ask. I move across to my bed and sit on the edge, watching him.

He startles a little at my voice, but nothing extreme. He was alert, expecting me. Some rational part of my brain is aware this is simply because it is my room, but I like to imagine he is a little scared of me. "Busy," he answers. "Yours?"

Did he sound informal just now or is that my imagination? I stand up and cross to him. Since he is still sitting on the floor, I tower over him. I use this to my advantage, leaning in and looking menacing. I drop my voice to a deeper octave and speak slowly, the way I've heard my father do countless times before. "I have been busy attending to the duties befitting the prince of your realm."

I watch the muscles in his neck twitch as he swallows. Fear crosses his face. It's like a drug, fear. It fills the veins of the person who feels it and changes their behavior. I have been that person on many occasions. But fear is also a drug to those who cause it. I can feel it flowing in me now. I have the power to influence the life of this boy. I feel it like fire flowing through me. It's mine to wield and control. I let the fear linger in the air without speaking for a few heartbeats. Neither of us moves.

Finally, I lean back and take a deep breath. "I need to go to strength training before dinner. Is that something you'd like to witness?" I ask, my voice taking on a slightly friendlier tone. I don't need this child to hate me. I need this child to remember who I am and fear me enough to respect me.

"If that's where you would like me to be," Toby answers. I still hear the fear quavering in his voice. I resist the urge to smile at it.

"Follow me." I walk quickly, testing his ability to keep up. I am halfway down the hall before I stop and turn. I'm pleasantly surprised to see that he is only a few steps behind me. I snap my fingers. "I forgot my training bar. It is under the bed in my room. Would you run back, grab it, and bring it out to the front lawn?" I turn back around and continue toward my training without waiting for a response.

The bar we often use for training is not heavy, by our standards, but it is also not light. In Sarcheda we lift blocks in competitions. Each block is carefully crafted to weigh the same and be the same shape. They are made out of a type of rock mixed with dirt and other substances. In training, we will lift the blocks above our heads. The average adult can lift six. My father is the current champion in the competitions, he can lift eleven. The bar we often use to practice our form and strengthen our muscles weighs more than one block but less than two blocks. Toby, although he is less than ten annuals, should be able to lift it. Carrying it, however, will be a challenge. I am testing him with this request. I want to see what he is capable of. But I also want to see how far he is willing to push himself.

My trainer and Marcus are standing together on the front lawn of my family home when I push open the door. Most people in our realm have a strength training regiment, but mine is always public. This is because my training is important to our people. There are big expectations that I will one day surpass my father in lifting. It is something I have yet to be able to live up to. But today is not about blocks. Today is about muscle development. Today is about form.

"Where is your bar?" my trainer barks from his position on the wall surrounding my family home. He is leaning back, his legs crossed at the ankles. Besides my father, he is the strongest man in Sarcheda. He consistently loses by only one block to my father. I have never seen him attempt the number of blocks my father wins competitions with. I have never seen anyone attempt that number. Sometimes I wonder if that is because my father is truly stronger or if it is because they know better than to attempt to beat the king.

"My personal servant is bringing it. I was in a hurry and forgot to grab it," I answer. My voice is loud and carries to the few people who have assembled from around Sarcheda. My practice time coincides with many people leaving their shops for the day to head home. Again, this is not an accident. Marcus has worked my schedule to maximize the time I am visible.

I notice many of the people in attendance today are young women. This is a trend that started when I surpassed my tenth annual and became fully mature. Soon I will reach the fifteenth, the final age marker affecting all citizens of Fraun. By that point, people will expect me to begin searching for a mate. There is no shortage of women in Fraun who want to be Sarcheda's next princess.

I take my time walking to the trainer, who pushes himself off the wall but doesn't come to me. "We'll begin with the push-offs," he commands.

I do not argue. This training is the only thing that keeps me on the path to becoming stronger than my father. It is my destiny. I put my arms out, ready to drop into position on the ground. Marcus lays his hand on my elbow and leans in. "Shirt," he whispers.

This is new, which is why I always forget it. I am a prince in Sarcheda. Now that I am fully mature by our standards, it is customary for me to appear in public settings such as this shirtless, with my bare chest on display. The custom began as a way for citizens to judge the muscles and strength of the rulers. I pull my shirt off and cast it to the side.

Then I drop into position for push-offs, parallel to the ground, supported by my hands and toes. My palms are flat on the ground, directly under my shoulders. I bend my elbows, bringing my nose down close to the dirt. Then I straighten them again, pushing off the ground. I do this with controlled speed fifteen times.

"Right hand up," the trainer barks.

I turn my left palm in to better support my weight and bring my right hand up to the small of my back. In this manner, I continue pushing off the ground for a count of fifteen.

"Left hand up," the trainer barks. I seamlessly change hands and do another fifteen count.

By the time I jump up to my feet, Toby is there. My training bar is beside him, one end on the ground and the other in his hand. He looks almost like he is leaning on it, but otherwise, he doesn't look tired at all. I'm impressed he was able to get this down here that quickly and not look out of breath. But I control myself, being sure not to let any pride for him show on my face.

I cross to him and take the bar. "Where do you want me?" he asks quietly.

"Control the crowd," I tell him. Truly there aren't many people here today. But I need to see what this boy can do with a small assembled group. I need to see what he thinks I mean when I ask him to control them. He nods once and heads in that direction. I bring the bar to the trainer.

"Slow and steady twenty count," he tells me.

I drop onto the ground, this time on my back. I hoist the bar over my chest, one hand positioned at either end. I push my arms out until they're fully extended and do a slow twenty count in my head. Then I bring the bar back down until it is hovering just over my chest. Again, a slow twenty count. I repeat this three more times, never moving quickly and never jerking the bar. My goal here is to make this look simple, although the muscles in my arms twitch and beg me to rush the process. The citizens watching should think this is easy. Then, when they try it on their own, they'll feel the pain and the burn in their muscles. In this way, they learn their prince's strength.

When this is done, I feel the trainer's hands on the end of the bar. "Release," he says. I do just that, unwrapping my fingers from the material and allowing him to take the weight. Then I jump to my feet in one fluid motion. I push myself to stand and see a small nod from my trainer, he is pleased with our progress. He will give me further notes after the session when the public has been released. "You running today?" he asks.

I nod. Running is not a requirement of my training. He always leaves this up to me. Today I feel like a good run. I have been cooped up in the house all day, pretending to be busy with a full schedule. I'd much prefer to spend the next few minutes burning off energy in a real way. I crane my neck first to my right shoulder and then to my left, stretching my neck. I pull my arms behind my back, feeling that satisfying pull on the shoulder. Then I pull my leg up behind me, stretching those muscles. Finally, I rise to the balls of my feet and bounce a little.

I notice Toby has gathered the young women in the group into an arc and is talking to them. Their eyes are still on me, but I wonder what he is saying. What promises is he making? I smile a little as I take off in a sprint. I have a feeling this boy will work out after all. First day on the job and he's already making the ladies happy.

Chapter 3

The run around the outskirts of town is the closest thing to peaceful I ever experience in my hectic life. Once I'm beyond the houses the grass grows taller because Fraunians don't walk here. It's that kind of quiet you get when you are the only living being around. Not silent, but lacking any of our noise. I can hear the wind rustling the grass and I can hear my breathing. I concentrate on the steps, counting them as my feet slam the ground. I am not wearing shoes today so I don't travel further out into the grass. Instead, I stay near the closest thing to a path.

The ravine pops up on my right. I know it's coming and yet it's still a surprise. I run along its edge, looking down into the depths. This ravine, which marks the border at the edge of Sarcheda and Fraun, is deep. I can see the rocks that make up the sides, but I cannot see the floor. I stay far enough away from the edge to keep myself safe and yet close enough to taunt death. It is my way of proving to myself that I am daring.

If I were to keep running in this direction I would eventually reach Castle Fraun, which is housed in

Renchenda. I hate that it's in Renchenda. It's the biggest, best building we have. It was built by Fraunian hands during the time of Oberian the Second.

So why was it given to Renchenda, the realm known for wisdom, to maintain? They should be housing our maps and family trees. They don't need the largest stone structure Fraun has ever built. They don't need a symbol of strength jutting out above the landscape of their realm. We need that. That castle should belong to Sarcheda. That castle should belong to me.

I notice my speed has increased with my anger and I focus for a few breath cycles on bringing myself back on track. The sun is hitting the horizon now, which means I will be late for dinner if I don't head back. I turn myself and head back to my family home.

Toby is still standing by the wall, a group of girls from Sarcheda standing with him. They spot me and their posture instantly gets rigid and formal. One girl, with yellow hair, feels comfortable enough to wave. I don't return the gesture. I stand in front of them but continue to run in place. I know the moment I stop my muscles will feel the burn and fatigue of the run. I'm not ready to deal with that yet.

"Prince Tin," Toby greets, "these ladies were hoping to take up a minute of your time."

I take my time looking around at the faces of the four girls who have waited for an audience with me.

Perhaps they stayed because they were interested in Toby, but now that they have realized he can cause me to pause they are no longer paying attention to him. They are all near my age and pretty. They all have long hair, which is common in Fraun. Our hair ceases to grow when we reach fifteen annuals. It is a sign of our maturity. These girls have it.

I bite down on my tongue to keep my smile in check. "Speak quickly, I have a dinner to get to," I bark. These girls didn't wait for pleasantries. Toby is pleasant. They wanted strength. I can do that.

"I wanted to invite you to a dinner at my house, Majesty," the yellow-haired girl who waved says. "I am learning to cook and I am sure I could offer you something that would please you." She makes a point of pushing her arms together in a way that squeezes her flesh up and out of her dress.

"Why would I dine with your family?"

"Because we can offer you the best vegetables in the land. Our farm often supplies food for your kitchens," she answers, batting her eyelashes at me.

I scoff. "My kitchen has a chef of the highest caliber. If we are to dine together I will invite you here." I look beyond her to the other women. "What else can I do for you, ladies?"

There is silence in the clearing. I let it spread out. Then I offer them a full smile. I'm always surprised at how well this works. The girls, probably ready to hate me for being rude merely a heartbeat before this, are now smiling and melting again in front of my eyes. "Good day, ladies," I say. I give a shallow bow to them and they melt even further at the ironic gesture.

Then, before the girls can say anything else, I resume my jog and head back into my family's home. I can hear stomps behind me and I imagine it's Toby. When I'm inside the door, I finally stop moving. My heart is pounding, my legs are warm, and I'm breathing heavily. I turn to face Toby. "That went well," I say.

"They had some things they wanted to ask you about," he says. "Things that they're concerned about. Things a prince may be able to help with."

I scoff. "Like what?"

"There isn't always enough food for their families. Sometimes they worry that they'll go hungry. Some buildings need to be remade, like the school. They want the prince to help them get these things fixed."

It is too bold for a servant who has been in my employ for only one sun. I narrow my eyes at him. "What, exactly, did you think I was going to do about those problems?"

He seems to understand my anger and shuffles his feet nervously. "I don't know."

I take two slow steps toward Toby until we are close enough that I could reach out and slap him for the overstep.

I don't. Instead, I stand there silent until he grows uncomfortable and fidgets. His arms flinch at his sides and his hands clench and unclench. Finally, I lean my weight back away from him a little and offer him a smile. "I have heard the concerns before. Unfortunately, I am not King. Were I King, perhaps I could take these concerns to the council and discuss them, maybe even help find a solution. But, as a Prince, I am not allowed in that council room any more than you are. You know that, don't you?"

He nods, still nervous about me being this close. I like that he is scared of me. I want him to remember who I am and what kind of power I have. "Someday, I will be King. Then I will be able to do something about the concerns of my people."

He visibly swallows. "So you'll listen to concerns when you are King?" he asks.

I lean in close like I'm sharing a secret. He flinches, but I ignore it. "If they're important people with important concerns, of course."

Then I straighten myself and take my sore legs and sweaty body to my room to clean up for dinner. In that interaction, I had the power. Soon I will be sitting down to dinner with my father, the actual King. In that one, I certainly will not. I must prepare myself for that other role.

Chapter 4

"Y ou're late," my father's voice echoes around the dining room. I try not to flinch and fail. He notices. "Oh, did I scare the little prince?" he asks in a high-pitched tone meant to sound like a baby.

I drop into an empty chair halfway down the table. My mother is seated at the end farthest from the fireplace. She is wearing a thick shawl, a bored blank expression, and cold eyes. There's steam coming from the bowl of soup in front of her. "I can't be that late, mother's soup is still warm," I say.

In my house, you stand up to the king. That is the one way to earn his respect. He believes that if you have something to say, you say it. Of course, you'll often find yourself punished for your opinion. But punishment for being strong is better than punishment for being weak.

Father laughs. The sound is entirely too joyous for the image we're projecting. Three people sitting uncomfortably around a table that could easily fit six bodies. Three empty chairs that, to my knowledge, are never used. Cold stone room, warm crackling fire. None of this screams jovial dinner meeting. Yet, my father is laughing. I suppose that means he is in a good mood. I wonder why. Did he have a meeting that went well? Did he go hunting today and catch something?

A woman appears from the kitchen entrance and places a bowl of soup in front of me. I look down at it, stirring it around with my spoon to see what is in it. It looks like it may be an earthworm stew. We had earthworms yesterday, meaning he didn't go hunting. If father had caught something on his hunting trip, he would have made sure that animal was prepared for dinner. Even if that meant changing the entire menu and throwing away what had already been prepared. His pride and bragging rights are more important than saving food.

I take a bite and the taste confirms my thoughts. It's earthworm stew and it tastes as if it has been marinating in flavor for some time. This was prepared yesterday.

To my right, my mother takes a bite of her stew. She's not careful and the sound of her slurp fills the room. I close my eyes, anticipating his wrath. "Can't you eat without slurping like a commoner?" he bellows. The table rocks as if it too were flinching away from the king of strength. "I know you were raised in a common household and have no royal blood, but you don't have to remind me of it at every single meal."

"I'm sorry," my mother answers delicately. Her voice is a shadow of his. "It was an accident. It won't happen again."

"Yes, it will." But he says it with a dismissive wave. There are days when this is something he is willing to fight endlessly about. There are days when he is incapable of letting something like this go. It seems like tonight he is willing to forgive.

I shoot my mother a look that I hope she takes as it was intended, to mean "be more careful." I doubt the king will be as forgiving the second time.

"I hear you approved the hiring choice for your new security man," Father says.

"Servant," I correct. I take a bite of stew to keep myself from looking at him to see if he takes offense to this correction.

"Is that what we are to call him?" he asks. He doesn't sound offended. I risk a look. He's smiling.

"Well, I'm sure he would answer to 'servant'. His name, however, is Toby." The king's smile falters just a little.

"He is not to be a friend of yours. That is not why we are providing him food and a roach to ride."

So this is how they are paying the boy. I had wondered. I assumed he was being paid with a room in the house. Evidently, I was wrong. It is common practice to provide servants in the royal home with housing in exchange for their work. It is also common practice to provide them with food for themselves or their families.

Providing a roach to someone just to give them transportation to and from their place of work is not as common. Roaches are alive. They are employees of my family themselves. My father is paying for my servant with the services of one of his. I'm certain that is intentional, to make me feel as though my servant wouldn't be possible without his. It's a power move.

"I don't need a friend," I say. "I need a servant." I take another bite of stew, hoping my forced calm is its own form of power move.

"I'd like to meet this boy." He claps his hands and the woman who brought my stew pops back out of the door. She is behind him so quickly I can only assume she was standing there with her ear to the door waiting to be summoned. "Bring me the servant named Toby," he commands.

She bows. "As you wish," she answers. It's his required answer to everything from the people who work in our home. With those three words, she has given me fear. I didn't take the time today to prepare Toby for speaking with my father. I didn't tell him to answer any command with this phrase. I didn't tell him to bow deep and full bows before the king. If he thought I was someone to be feared this afternoon, he will not be ready for my father who makes me look as scary as a commoner from Enchenda.

I wonder what happens if my servant quits before the end of his first night on the job. Would I get another one? Would he survive another fortnight after displeasing the king?

The door that leads to the hallway at the front of the house opens and Toby's quiet footsteps cross the room. "Majesty," he greets. I'm relieved to see him drop into a full bow. "You wished to speak with me."

"I hear that your name is Toby and you are to be the servant to my son here. Is that true?"

"If it pleases you, Majesty." Good answer, Toby. This kid must really be Sarcheda. He knows the stories of the king.

"Tell me, servant, do you think my son would punish you if you were to make a mistake?"

This is a test. It's not a test of Toby, although he likely thinks it is. This is a test of me. Have I been able to ensure, in just one sun, that this boy believes I will punish him if he errs? Does he fear me? My father will accept no less. I force myself not to look at Toby. I cannot appear as though I am communicating with him right now. An eyebrow raise, a glare, or any gesture that could be considered an exchange of information will be punished. Because, if this question were for me, I know the right answer. Do I feel like a misstep will bring the wrath of the king down on me? Absolutely. The king wants me to mirror that same behavior and draw that same fear.

"He seems to have high expectations of me, sir," Toby answers. "I have yet to make a mistake."

"But when you do," Father continues, "how do you believe that will be handled?"

"I would expect to be punished accordingly for letting Prince Tin down, Majesty."

"I see," Father answers. He takes a bite of his stew. Then he takes another. He has not dismissed Toby, but he also is clearly done with this conversation. This is another test. Will Toby wait to be dismissed, speak out of turn, or assume? One right choice and two wrong.

"You're dismissed," I say in a loud voice. I wave my hand toward the door Toby came in. He nods and heads out.

When the door closes with an audible click my father clears his throat. "I was under the impression I was king of this realm," he says.

"You are. Surely you'd want your son to demonstrate power and control with his servant without having to come to you." I force my shoulders up and down in a casual gesture that doesn't feel at all casual. Inside I'm quaking with fear. I can only hope it doesn't show.

"That was not real power. That was a copy of my power. You mimic my actions when you want to show power. You have none of your own. That is a sign of real weakness."

I feel something new bubbling inside. Anger. Anger directed at my father. I feel it boil in my veins and decide to embrace it. "If it is a weakness to act like you, perhaps that is a reflection of you."

My mother's intake of breath is sharp.

The king's eyes narrow dangerously. "What did you say to me?" he growls.

I meet his gaze and, careful not to copy his actions, widen my eyes. "You heard me," I challenge. Anger, apparently, makes me do stupid things. I know punishment is coming. I can see it brewing in his eyes. I think I'm ready. I prepare myself for all the options: he may rise from the chair and smack me, he may force me to kiss his feet, he may demand I leave the room, or he may berate me. I tell myself I can handle all of it.

"Leave him alone." His eyes leave my face and flick to my mother's at the sound of her voice.

"Idiot," I whisper. Because she is. Because I can handle his wrath but she cannot. We know this. We have seen her lose a baby, bruise herself so badly she can't go in public, and even have to see the medicine tent to right a bone. She is no match for the king of strength.

"Tin, show your mother what happens when she sticks her nose in men's business," my father says.

My stomach plummets. This is how he will punish me. He wants me to punish her. I wasn't ready for that. I look at my mother, frail and small in that chair. She is nothing, not really. She can throw her head back and lift her chin in public, putting on the air of someone royal. But she's nothing when no one is around. She usually just sits there, silent as a servant. What would I have to punish her for?

Of course, she did just speak up. Had she just kept her mouth shut we wouldn't be in this situation. I would be dealing with a punishment that I can handle, instead of this.

But I can handle this, I tell myself. I stand up, my chair scraping along the rock. My mother looks at me, her eyes pleading. "Don't take it too far," she says. She's speaking quietly as if she can deliver the words directly to me and leave him out of it. As if this wasn't his idea. As if this wasn't him controlling me like you control roaches for travel.

I step closer to her, raising my hand. I know what I have to do. It's easy. I've seen father do it hundreds of times. All I have to do is slap her. One should be enough to show him I'm not afraid. Once is enough to show strength. Too much and I would quickly become the boy who is assaulting my father's wife, the queen. Too much and he would have to step in and defend the idea of her honor.

If I know what I have to do, why is my arm locking in place? Why can't I finish it? My hand is shaking with effort as if someone strong were holding my forearm to prevent me from slapping her.

"Do it," she whispers. Her eyes twitch to check on Father. I don't look. I can tell by the fear on her face when her eyes return to me that he is still angry. He means to see this through.

I hear his chair scrape, just a little. If I don't do this, he will. He will do it worse than I ever would. I let my hand fly. I hear the noise of the contact and feel the sting in my fingers. A cry escapes her and it cuts right through me.

I don't apologize, because that would show weakness.

I don't wait to be dismissed. I just leave the room.

I'm suddenly weighed down by the inescapable truth of my new reality. I just took one step up the ladder, by gaining a servant and standing up to my father. That new step will cost me. I will never again be the boy I was this morning.

It's time I grew up.

Chapter 5

One Annual Later

"Toby," my shout echoes across the empty room. I imagine it traveling out the open door, down the stone hallway, and finding Toby's ears. He was not at my strength training this morning. I did not see him at lunch, although I did notice that everything was cleaned up from breakfast. I did not see him during my tutoring session with Marcus or after, although my change of clothes was lying on the bed ready for me. He was not at my afternoon strength training either. Now, coming back from my run and dripping with sweat, he is still nowhere to be found. My servant seems to have adopted a new strategy: be neither seen nor heard.

Marcus comes into the room. I keep a stern look on my face and narrow my eyes at him. "Where is Toby?" I demand. "I haven't seen him all day."

"Is there a reason you are yelling, sir?" Marcus asks. "Surely if your father heard you yelling for your servant he would assume you have no control over the boy, yes?"

He's not wrong. "Where is he?" I press.

"I believe he was in the kitchen. Would you like me to have him sent up?"

"Yes," I answer. "Tell him to hurry." In reality, I have nothing I need Toby for. But why is he avoiding me? That cannot be allowed.

Marcus leaves the room and I pull off my pants and throw them on the floor. From the wooden cabinet at the side of my room, I pull out a clean pair. Like the ones on the floor and all of the pairs nestled in the cabinet, this pair is black. I do have a pair of red ones, which is the color associated with Sarcheda, somewhere in the house. They are tailor-made to fit me snuggly and are worn on important occasions for the realm. I hate wearing them if I don't have to. I much prefer the softer fabric, tie waist, and snug ankles of these black pants.

Just as I get them tied around my waist, the door opens. "You were looking for me," Toby says. He bows. He has been in my employment for an annual. He has made mistakes which he has been punished for. But lately, he seems like he spends his days avoiding me.

I point to the discarded pants on the floor. "Take care of those," I tell him. "I want them clean before I need them again."

I see his eyes flick up to the cabinet. Likely he sees the numerous other pairs there, ready and waiting. He says nothing. Instead, he crosses the room and bends down to retrieve them. I chose this moment when he is bent over with his fingers barely grazing the pants, to take a step forward.

It's not a fast movement. It's just one slow step in his direction. But at the movement of my foot, he flinches. A smile spreads over my face. "Do I scare you, Toby?" I ask.

My new-found power, the power to scare people with my words and punish people who step out of line, courses through my veins. I understand why my father treats people the way he does. Not only do people do what you ask when they fear you, they give you space by staying out of your way. No one in Sarcheda would dare question me now that I am fifteen. I am, by all measurements we use, an adult. It makes me even more dangerous.

Toby doesn't answer, which I suppose is wise. There isn't an answer he could have given to that question that I wanted to hear. His eyes, which he'd closed just a little with that flinch, told me everything I needed to know.

There are a couple of short taps on my bedroom door and then the door is pushed open. Marcus is standing in the doorway. I dismiss my servant with a simple wave of his hand. He is merely steps beyond the door when Marcus explains the reason for his interruption. "I'm sorry to bother you again, Prince Tin, but your father needed me to remind you that you are to have a date for dinner tomorrow evening. Do you need me to procure a date for you when I am in town later tonight?"

I groan. The dinner date tomorrow is the kind of thing I pretend I forgot about in hopes that it will go away. I am barely fifteen annuals. In Fraun, this means I'm completely grown and expected to start finding my family. This is even more urgent because of my royal blood, as my father insists. It is imperative that I find a spouse and give us enough time to have a male heir before we need someone else to rule. Father hasn't mentioned this dinner date in almost a fortnight, since he put down the silly requirement. I had hoped he'd forgotten. I certainly haven't been on the hunt for someone to bring to dinner. "Find me someone, anyone," I tell Marcus.

He nods. "As you wish."

"Wait," I say, holding up a single finger. I close my eyes and sigh. "Find me someone near my age who is shorter than my height and isn't bad to look at."

"Should they also be from a respectable family, sir?" Marcus asks. His tone of voice tells me he knows what a ridiculous list I have given him. If such a girl existed in Sarcheda I'd already know about her. He's being ludicrous by adding another tough expectation to the list.

I glare at him. "Of course. Don't bring me the daughter of a roach trainer if a shop owner's daughter is available." I hope my wide eyes are daring him to speak out.

Instead, he bows. "As you wish, Majesty."

He slips out of the room and I drop onto the edge of the bed and flop backward, throwing my arms out at my sides. I've been thinking lately about what it will be like to rule Sarcheda. Really rule it. It's something I can't truly imagine because I'm not allowed to sit in on the council meetings so I don't know what happens there. I assume my father must try to dominate the meetings since he's the king of the first realm.

Sarcheda has held the first realm designation since it was taken away from Renchenda, the realm known for wisdom, because of something nefarious in their past. Marcus tells me this has been the case for almost every realm in the course of our history. They've all had their chance to rule and they've all lost it because of some terrible decision that goes against the council and embarrasses Fraun.

I've learned these mistakes and studied them under Marcus' guidance. Enchenda was the first realm to lose the title. Their Queen's sister had a baby out of wedlock. This was early in our history when the expectation was a quick marriage ceremony before you pop out an infant. From this, I am to learn the lesson that things kept quiet cannot be used against you, especially if you are in the first realm. For this reason, when my mother gave birth to a baby girl last annual, the baby simply disappeared. Girls are not needed to rule Sarcheda. If something were to happen to me it would be better to find someone else from our realm willing and able to lead than to hand it to a baby sister.

Marchenda earned the title of First Realm after it was taken from Enchenda. They had a good run but it was brought to an end in the dumbest way I've heard of. The king of the realm turned grey and had no heirs. This was a grievous mistake on behalf of the council. I imagine them discussing his age saying things like "why shouldn't he be allowed to continue ruling into his grave?" Or "Worry about it after he's gone." From this lesson, I learned that someone with a strong will needs to lead that council. Someone willing to tell them when they're being ridiculous and influence them to change their silly policies. A ruler to replace that one should have been lined up long before his death. A plan should have been in place, especially for the first realm.

This is when Renchenda earned the first realm title. The grievance with their ability to lead came from a more interesting tale. A child was born to the great-niece of the seated King. This woman was not married. It looked like the title of First Realm would be stripped away from them, as it had been in Enchenda. But King Spec, the only King who sounds like he had a spine over there in Renchenda, argued. He claimed the girl was not living in his home and was not a direct relation to him. He promised to get more control over her and stop it from happening again. He convinced the council to let Renchenda keep their title. After the birth of her second child out of wedlock, the girl mysteriously disappeared. It makes me laugh just to think about how shocked the council must have been. The girl in question is suddenly gone, overnight? I'm sure there was an investigation. Marcus says this is a time when everything would have gone to chaos. A seated King surely would've been suspected of murder. Rather than deal with the trial and all the pain it could cause, Renchenda themselves suggested the title of First Realm be passed along.

That was when Sarcheda became the first realm for the first time in history.

I intend to learn from the mistakes of my predecessors and keep that title.

I don't intend to be perfect. No one could be as perfect as these rules suggest. Things happen. No, my plan makes a lot more sense than that.

I intend to never be caught.

Chapter 6

I meet my dinner date in the front entrance hall just before taking her into the dining room. I look her up and down, appraising her form and outfit. She is shorter than me by about a click. Her hair falls past her shoulders in careful braids. Her skin is gorgeously dark and smooth. The outfit she has chosen, a red dress that exposes her shoulders, is perfect for a dinner in the royal home of Sarcheda. Our house color, after all, is red.

I smile at her and reach out to take her hand. I bring it to my lips, kissing it lightly. "Good evening," I greet, holding her eyes.

She smiles shyly. "Good evening, Majesty. My name is Naomi."

I drop her hand but not her gaze. "How old are you, Naomi?"

"Fourteen annuals."

I hold out my elbow and she threads her limb through mine. I begin to lead her toward the hallway to the dining room. "My father will expect you to answer a lot of questions tonight, I'm sorry for that." I give her a little pout. "He is very controlling. What does your father do for a living?"

"He owns the market in the town square."

"Wonderful. That makes you quite high on the social ladder, does it not?"

Her bare shoulder rises and falls. "It makes my father high on the ladder, I suppose."

No good. I cannot have this beautiful girl playing demure and quiet to my father. He likes loud and proud. "Take pride in your place in our society," I say. I stop in the hallway and turn to face her. I use my free hand to lift her chin. "You are a beautiful young woman from a respectable family who is on a date with the Prince of Sarcheda." A smile turns her cheeks up, making her even more beautiful. "Are you happy to be here?"

"I'm honored to be here," she answers.

"Good. Let us make this a night you'll never forget." I wink at her and she casts her eyes down in an adorable way that makes me think she may be a little embarrassed. But, somehow, it's not a bad thing. It's not like an embarrassment made to make me feel like I messed up. Somehow it feels… powerful.

I shake my head, clearing my thoughts. "We should get in there before my father comes looking for us." I decide I'll try the wink again, later. See how she reacts. Perhaps this is a move I can use with women in the realm, something they like. I'll have to keep that in mind.

My mother is already sitting in her chair, her eyes blurry and unfocused but pointed toward the fire roaring in the fireplace on her side. Her hands are fixed on her lap. Her shoulders are curled in on themselves as if she has a bubble wrapped around her pushing her tighter into herself. I lay a hand on her shoulder. "Queen Alexa," I speak quietly trying to draw her attention to the moment without scaring her.

She blinks rapidly like she is waking from a dream. Her eyes find my face and she smiles. She brings her hand up to lay over mine. "My son."

"I want you to meet someone." I tip my head toward the girl behind me. "This is Naomi, she is joining us for dinner tonight."

My mother's eyes dart quickly around the room. I get the distinct feeling she is making sure father is not here. Then her eyes land on Naomi, taking her in. "Hello, my dear." She lets go of my shoulder and reaches out a hand. "Welcome to our home."

Naomi bends into a full bow, taking my mother's hand and pressing her lips to it in one smooth gesture. "Your Majesty, thank you for having me. This is truly a beautiful home."

My mother frees her hand from Naomi and waves it carelessly around the room. "The ancestors built it and the servants maintain it. I can take no responsibility," she says.

"Tin, take your seat. Your father will be along shortly and we don't want to anger him, now do we?"

"Of course not," I say. Although, some days, I want nothing more than to get him fired up. I look forward to the day when I can truly give him a taste of his own medicine. It's coming, I can feel it. He just doesn't know it yet. I will be the one who makes him pay for the way he has treated my mother and me. But today is not that day. So I hold out the chair on my mother's left for Naomi. Then I walk around the table and take the other side chair. "I hope you're hungry," I say. "Our chef is amazing."

"How old are you, Naomi?" my mother inquires.

"Fourteen, milady."

"So you are of the age to have children."

Naomi's mouth falls open and sputters like an open door in a strong breeze. I jump in to rescue her. "It's our first date, mother. It seems a bit early to be discussing such things."

"You are the prince. Do you think the king will not mention it? At least I was kind about it." My mother pouts in my direction, clearly upset that I didn't see her rude question as a kind gesture.

We don't have time to debate it further because the door opens and the king enters. "Good evening family and guest," he bellows. He is using that deep, fake voice he uses when he speaks to crowds as if the room is full instead of housing one table and three people. He's set to impress tonight. I suppose that may work to my advantage because it implies he cares what this young girl who is joining me for dinner thinks of him. He may decide to be the best-behaved image of a king tonight. In other words, nothing like how he really is.

"Good evening, Majesty," Naomi says. She jumps out of her chair and bows fully before my father.

"Enough of that, you are at a dinner at my house. Be seated," father commands. They both take their seats. "Have you been waiting long?" he asks.

"We just arrived," I tell him.

"Perfect." He waves his hand in the direction of the kitchen and the servants scramble out carrying plates mounded with food. There are four servants tonight, one for each of us. The plate that is dropped in front of me smells like meat. Our most common foods around Fraun are vegetables and fruits because we grow them in our gardens. The personal garden for the royal family of Sarcheda is relatively large. We have a crew of at least five who tend to it. But meat is something we eat when it is available. It takes skill and strength to bring down most animals. I should have known father would take this as a perfect opportunity to show off the strength of Sarcheda.

I dip my utensil into the bowl and take a large bite. This is not an ant, but I'm not exactly sure what it is. I take another bite, testing out the flavors on my tongue. Before I can even swallow this second bite, my mother speaks up.

"What is this flavor I'm tasting?" she asks the servant who has set herself beside the kitchen door.

"I believe it is ladybug, Majesty."

I force myself to swallow and stare at my father in shock. Ladybugs are sentient beings, capable of speech and favors. They are not common insects, like ants. "Are you sure?" I ask. My eyes are on the king because he would have approved this menu.

"That is what I was told," the servant answers.

My father smiles and takes a large bite. He swallows with a satisfied sort of noise. "Delicious."

Naomi puts her spoon down. "With respect, Majesty, I'm not sure I can eat this. Ladybugs are common in the area around my house. I have spoken to a few of them and consider some of the young ones friends. It's not something I can consider food."

"Rest assured," the king says, "we did not murder this creature. She passed of natural causes and was gifted to our chef by the ladybug community. We have their blessing to dine on this meat tonight." He takes another bite as if to punctuate his statement.

I notice he is the only one of us who is eating it now that we all know what it is we were served. I set my utensil down beside my bowl. "If you are uncomfortable, I can take you home." I hold my hand out to Naomi. "Would you like to take a walk with me?"

She smiles gratefully and places her hand in mine.

Together, we stand. She bows her head at my mother and then my father. "Thank you for having me in your beautiful home."

"You are seriously going to leave food in those bowls?" Father asks. His voice takes on a dangerous tone that I recognize. "The bug is already dead. Children in Fraun are starving and would kill for that meal. You are going to leave this house with that bowl of food left uneaten?"

I drop Naomi's hand and take her bowl from the table. I dump the contents into my bowl, filling it to the brim. Then I pick it up in both of my hands and smile at my father. "We will eat it as we walk," I say. I put my lips to the bowl and pretend to take a sip. "I think it's a nice night for a walk."

I am pushing my luck here and I know it. But, as Marcus is always teaching me, any opportunity to use someone's weakness against them should be taken. My father wants to show strength to his guest, which is a weakness of his character tonight. My father is seldom vulnerable and right now, he is. I smile at him. "Thank you for understanding that we'd like a little time to be alone," I say. He won't argue with that.

Naomi takes my elbow and we head out of the house. I steer us toward the stables. "Where are we going?" Naomi asks. "I live the other direction."

"My father should never have served that meat," I

say. "I'm sorry it offended you. It offended me." At the stables, I knock on the wood. "Hello," I call out. "Is anyone here?"

A roach scurries out of the darkness. "The boy prince," he speaks slowly and low as if he thinks I am stupid.

I hold out the bowl. "Someone found a ladybug and used it to make stew. I am not in favor of that species being used in a recipe, as I am not a fan of roaches being used in that way. However, I cannot bring the creature back to life by refusing to eat it. Would anyone here be interested in the stew?"

His antennae move around as if he is smelling the bowl I am holding out. "Will you handle the necessary punishment of whoever ordered this be prepared?" he asks, again in that slow speech.

I am well aware of who ordered this creature to be used in a meal served in my household. I am also aware of exactly what I would do if the chance to make him pay became available to me. "Absolutely," I answer.

"We will eat it. Leave it here."

I put the bowl down on the ground and offer Naomi my elbow. "Should we stop in the garden and help ourselves to some grapes?" I ask her.

"I'd love that," Naomi answers. She is practically purring. I played this evening perfectly to earn this beautiful woman's respect. She is practically eating out of my hand right now.

Tonight has been a perfect evening after all.

Chapter 7

The next morning I'm woken by the warmth of the rising sun spreading across my body. It takes me a few breaths to realize there is a weight on my shoulder and along the right side of my body. I open my eyes and look down at Naomi's mussed hair. That's right, I remember, last night I impressed the young maiden. Last night I learned that the stories of sharing a bed with someone, even if that bed is merely a bed of fallen leaves beside the river Fraun, are not underestimated.

I pull my arm out from underneath her head quickly. It shocks her awake. "Prince Tin," she mumbles. I see the look of shame cross her face and it makes me angry. Why would she be ashamed to awaken beside a prince? I jump to my feet as if this was a strength training exercise. I know the speed with which I complete this is impressive. Naomi flinches away from me, it makes me smile. "Are you afraid of me or embarrassed by what we did?" I challenge from my crouched position beside her. "I'm going to need you to pick one so I know how much anger to display."

"I didn't say either of those things," she answers.

Her voice is soft and shaky.

I lean in closer, putting my mouth beside her ear. "You didn't say either of those with your voice," I whisper. Then I pull back to see her face. "Lucky for us both, I am skilled in reading body language."

The muscles in Naomi's throat work as she swallows. Small beads of sweat break out on her upper lip. She blinks rapidly. I wink at her. "It's also lucky for you that your fear is something I find particularly satisfying." I run my hand along her arm. "The satisfaction calms my anger."

Naomi sighs. "I'm sorry if I angered you at all, Prince. I woke up this morning and forgot where I was. It was jarring to wake up in the tangled grass." She flashes me a smile. "This is not something I normally wake up to find." She gestures around her. "Do you happen to know where my dress might be?"

I look around the area and find a pile of clothing just out of arm's reach. "I would assume it is in that pile." I push myself to a full standing position and stretch. Then I walk to the pile and free her dress from under my clothing. I throw it in her direction and proceed to pull on my pants. There is a shirt here in the pile because when we left my father's house I was dressed for dinner. In many circumstances, those that are not formal, Sarcheda citizens would not need a shirt. Certainly, the prince of strength wouldn't require one. I take it in my fist but do not slip it on. Then I spin to find Naomi standing nearby with her dress hastily thrown on. She is looking down at her feet.

"Well, it's been fun," I tell her, "but I have places to be."

She nods. "Will I see you again?"

"Perhaps," I say. This brings her eyes up to me. I can see unasked questions in them. Things she is afraid to say to her prince. I smile. "If it suits me to be seen with you, I will let you know." I know I am being cruel. But my answer is honest. The prince of the realm should only be seen with a woman who is befitting of his status. I have to think about whether this woman is the kind of citizen who I should be seen with. I have a lot of thinking to do. "For now, I am going to take a walk." She takes a step in my direction as if intending to come with me. "Alone," I add.

She freezes. For a heartbeat the expression on her face is sadness. Then she smiles. "You know best, Majesty."

"I certainly do," I tell her. Then I turn my back on the first woman I've ever been intimate with and walk away in the direction of the river Fraun and Enchenda.

It's a nice day today. The sun is shining and the singing birds are far enough off to not pose a threat to me and my safety. If I'm quiet, which I'm careful to be, I can hear the river Fraun bubbling away in the distance. I follow the noise. Walking in the woods is strange. I feel a sense of odd calm out here that I have never felt before. There's no one to control, there's no one to watch for power moves. It's just me and whatever wild animals may be hiding nearby, keeping their distance. It's calm and quiet. I hate it.

I pick up the pace, hoping to encounter something I can interact with. An angry animal would work. A Fraunian would be better. I push my way past a bunch of weeds and cut my skin on a tree branch, but the river comes into view.

I walk right up to the edge and crouch down. The water rushes through my fingers. It's cool but not too cold. I put my second hand in, cupping them together and letting them fill with liquid. Then I splash it on my face. I repeat the cupping motion, this time drinking the water. The water we use in my house is from this river. I suppose all the water for Fraun is from this river. I know there is a group that works the river, making sure the irrigation systems are all kept up and flowing nicely. I know there is also a team that works in my own house. But beyond that, I have no idea what goes into bringing this water to the people. Right this second, I'm not sure I care. Water has never tasted as clear and fresh as it does coming directly from the river.

I lie on the bank of the river and put my face directly in, drinking greedily. When I'm sure I can't take another sip, I push myself up to a sitting position and look around.

A girl is standing on the opposite bank, watching me with an amused expression on her face. She's young enough that I can't be sure if she's full height. Her hair is just barely grazing her shoulders. It is mostly brown although there are strands of it that look as though they are laced with the blood red of my realm. It's intriguing. She's intriguing. I offer her a smile. "Good morning."

She looks up at the trees above us and back down at me with a sort of bemused expression on her face. "It's afternoon," she says.

"Is it? I haven't been awake long. I must have overslept."

"Where are you from? Is your house near here?" She takes a step closer to the river. She is wearing pants made of a dark green material and a shirt that looks as though it is the same material just a few shades lighter. She is not wearing shoes, although that is pretty customary in Fraun. But the green coupled with the side of the river she is standing on gives me the impression that she is not from Sarcheda. She is likely from Enchenda.

"I am from Sarcheda. My house is not far from here. I just decided to go out and explore today. I don't get to see much of this area." I decide, suddenly, that this young girl will be easy to influence. I'll dangle a little power and influence in her direction and have her eating out of the palm of my hand. "My father probably wouldn't approve of me being here," I say quietly like it is a secret I'm offering to her. "He's very controlling, being the king and all."

Her face brightens as I expected it would. "You are

the prince of Sarcheda?"

"Guilty."

She surprises me then. She races forward, directly into the river. Her pants get wet practically to her knees, but she keeps running as if this is something she has done countless times. When she reaches the side of the bank I have been sitting on, quicker than I would have expected, she flops down beside me and holds out her hand. "I'm Princess Eselda of Enchenda," she says.

"Oh," my surprise causes my voice to freeze in my throat. It is the only word that will escape. The little princess. I had forgotten she existed. We are so isolated here in Fraun. I see Sarcheda citizens daily, but other citizens keep to their realms. I knew of her existence, but I have not seen her before today. Perhaps she will not be as easy to sway, I realize.

"Where is your house? What direction?" she asks.

I point off in the direction I came from this morning, assuming it is back that way. "How old are you?" I ask, trading a question for a question.

"Ten annuals. How old are you?"

"Fifteen. You have no siblings, correct?"

She squints at me and shakes her head. "Neither do you." We have both studied our history. "Is your father grey yet?" she asks.

Grey hair marks the death spiral for citizens of Fraun. No one with grey hair will last longer than five annuals. Grey hair sprouts from your head on the anniversary of your fortieth annual. "No, he has a few annuals before that happens. Is your father grey?" As a realm, I would think that would be concerning. This young girl is not fully grown yet. She is not an adult in our society. If she is the best Enchenda has to put on the throne, I'd imagine they are worried.

"No." She shrugs, giving the impression she doesn't care. Perhaps she knows it would be better for a strong Enchenda if she were a boy. "I don't know how old he is. Maybe I should ask him."

"What about your mother?" I ask.

Her face falls. For the first time since I met this little princess, her eyes lose their sparkle and look sad. I feel a pang in my chest, which catches me off guard. "My mother died," she says.

From the sadness, I would assume this death was recent. I don't remember hearing anything about a queen of Fraun dying. It seems like the kind of thing my father should have at least mentioned. Perhaps there were questionable circumstances. Perhaps she was killed. I decide not to ask. This young girl seems hurt by her past and, for reasons I cannot explain, I have no desire to hurt her further.

I decide not to stop myself from comforting her. I slip my arm over her shoulders. "I'm sorry you lost your mother," I say.

She sniffles and wipes her face. "It's alright. I'm getting used to it." I feel her pull away from me a little and I drop my arm. She smiles at me, showing me her brave face. "Do you have lessons with your tutor all the time?" Her eyes have some of their sparkle back now that she has resumed our question game.

"I do. His name is Marcus and I see him at least once a day."

"I don't have a tutor right now," she says. "My tutor stopped working at the house when my Mom died. I don't have another one yet."

"How are you getting your education?"

She shrugs. "Dad, a nice shopkeeper in town, and a bunch of old scrolls." She rolls her wet pant legs up, exposing the light, creamy skin of her calves. "I'm doing alright."

"I expect you are. You seem very smart for your age."

She glares at me again. I find I quite like this little glare of hers, the attitude behind it intrigues me. "You are not that much older than me, Prince."

Now it's my turn to shrug. "I suppose." I stretch my arms over my head. "I should probably head home. It was nice to meet you, Princess Eselda."

"Why are you here, anyway?"

For a heartbeat, I think about telling her the truth. I impressed a young woman from Sarcheda enough to convince her to sleep with me in the woods. I woke up this morning and decided I wanted to be alone. Then I walked to clear my head. I ended up right here and I'm intrigued by the blood-red highlights in your hair and the attitude behind your eyes so I'm talking to you even if you are from Enchenda and are entirely too young for me.

Instead, I smirk. "I will be king before long and I realized I should try to see more of Sarcheda. This is our border," I point to the river. "It made sense to travel over here and see it."

"You should come again, maybe leave Sarcheda and see other realms," she offers. "I can show you around Enchenda."

"Have you ever left Enchenda?" I ask, surprised to find myself interested in this answer. Perhaps it is only my father who keeps his child imprisoned inside his realm.

"No." She touches my shoulder. "But maybe I will."

I stand up and smile at this interesting little creature. "If you're ever in Sarcheda, find my house. Come by and we'll have a dinner large enough to impress you." I bow to her, turning up the charm. "Until then, milady, fair well."

She blushes and a giggle escapes from her mouth.

I hear that giggle in my head, like an echo, all the way back to my father's house.

Chapter 8

Spending the day out in the woods seemed like a good idea at the time. I felt powerful, unstoppable, and grown. Then I arrived home to an angry king. I was immediately confined to my room, a punishment that includes locks in this house. Dinner was not brought up to me, meaning the rumbling in my stomach was my only companion when I finally fell asleep. No one visited me all night. I was glad to not see my father, but it may have been nice to see my servant pop in to drop off food, start a fire, or explain what was happening in the rest of the house.

In the morning I wake to the sound of my bedroom door unlocking. I sit up, half expecting the visitor to be the king. Instead, Toby enters and shuts the door behind him. He delivers a tray of breakfast foods, lights a fire, and leaves quietly. I rise, stretching my back. Perhaps the punishment has run its course. After all, did I not display the strength my father is always searching for? Did I not give him a sense of pride by taking a maiden from the realm out? I settle in a chair in front of the fire and dig into the breakfast.

I don't hear the door to my room open or the footsteps crossing the room. My first indication that someone else has joined me is the slap I feel on the back of my head. My father's voice booms and echoes, amplified by the ringing in my ear. "You may think your title earns you respect in the realm but you will do well to remember that in this house you are my property."

I turned my face in his direction but kept my eyes down. "Majesty, I am truly sorry we were disrespectful. I was trying to earn favor with the young maiden and —"

"You should never invite a woman who wants you to disrespect a king into your bed. If she cannot show respect for the king of her realm, she will not show respect to you. Remember that." Father leans down close to me. "You are not worthy to be my successor. Every day you show me how immature you are." He spits and I feel the liquid drip on my cheek. It disgusts me, but I do not reach to wipe it off. "You will never disobey me or disappear like that again. Do I make myself clear?"

"Yes, Majesty," I answer. It must sound convincing because he stomps out of the room, leaving the door open. My ears are still ringing, but I refuse to react.

Marcus steps into the open doorway. "Prince Tin, it seems you have returned after all. You missed a lesson yesterday. I thought, perhaps, you were making running from your obligations a permanent life choice."

I sigh. "It was one lesson, Marcus. I'm here now."

"Good." He shuts the door, crosses to the chair across from me, and drops into it. "Let us go through the family tree," he says. He stretches out a parchment between us, directly on top of the remnants of my breakfast.

"Family trees?" I ask, my voice filled with skepticism. This is a lesson I do not need. It is a lesson I could probably give myself. I don't try to stifle the yawn that arises.

Marcus narrows his eyes. "Am I boring you with the lessons of your realm, Prince?"

"I didn't sleep well," I answer. "This lesson is one we have been through before. You better be gearing up to tell me something I don't know, Marcus."

"First, tell me the realms that have held the first seat on the council of kings."

I roll my eyes even as I answer. "Renchenda, Enchenda, Marchenda, Renchenda again, and then finally Sarcheda."

He paces before the fireplace. "Now tell me why, in your opinion, Renchenda was given the honor for a second time before we were ever allowed to hold the seat of power."

"Renchenda didn't have it long the first time," I say.

Marcus stops his pacing and turns. "Don't try to push the question away on a technicality, Majesty. Tell me why Fraun saw fit to give them the title of First Realm twice before honoring Sarcheda even once."

I sigh. "The council believes wisdom is valuable because it is with wisdom we can grow and learn." Anger bubbles in my stomach. I know I don't have to contain this anger, not in front of my tutor. He doesn't judge me. I let it all out. "That council is blind to the fact that wisdom is useless alone. They can come up with plans for fighting, but they need strength to win the battle. They can draw the blueprint for a house, but they need strength to build it. Renchenda having that first seat twice shows the council was blind to the fact that you need strength to get any task completed. They focused on the plan when they should have been focused on the execution."

Marcus smiles. "Good. Now tell me how you plan to keep the council from repeating this same mistake when you are king. Tell me how you will keep the rule of Fraun and the power seat in the hands of Sarcheda."

This is not something Marcus has ever asked me before. It gives me pause. Is there talk of taking the seat away from my father? What reason have they for considering that? Not for the first time, I hate that the council will not let me sit at the table. The anger bubbles to the surface of my skin and pours out of my mouth. "Are you telling me they talk of taking away the seat of Sarcheda?" I ask. "What right have they to do that? What has father done to deserve that? He cares for nothing as much as he cares for that council and their business. We worked hard for that seat and we work hard in honor of it. There is nothing Sarcheda cannot do."

"I agree, Majesty. But is strength enough alone? That is the question you must be able to answer for that council. That is the question they will ask you."

I stand and take a step closer to Marcus as if he were asking the question himself instead of trying to get me to think about it. "That old-fashioned council can either have Sarcheda in charge or they can have a realm without strength. That will be the ultimatum I give them," I answer.

"Do you mean to tell me you would leave Fraun and make a kingdom of your own if the council tried to vote to take away your seat?" Marcus asks, his eyes widening in surprise.

"That is exactly what I mean."

Marcus' eyes return to normal and he shakes his head. "You are being rash. How would you survive?"

I take a step back from him and consider what I've said. It takes me only a few seconds to come to the conclusion. "We would survive in the same way we always have. Tell me, what does that council do for us?"

"Well, we are stronger together, are we not?" Marcus lays a hand on my arm. "Think about the details before you go off yelling about a future you haven't imagined. Do you really think the council would let you walk away from that table?"

My shoulders sag. He's probably right, he's usually right. The council has convinced themselves and every citizen in Fraun that we are stronger as a unit. No one realm is supposed to become more powerful because the balance is what keeps us safe and happy. I shrug. "You tell me, Marcus. You know more than I do. What do we need the other realms for? What do they provide?"

He sighs. "Renchenda does bring a logic that is unmatched. In the face of dangers, it is Renchenda citizens who offer solutions that make the most sense. Marchenda, being the realm known for mirth, is the realm that keeps our history and stories of our past. If any realm were to keep us from making mistakes of the past, it would be them. Farcheda citizens are quick. They are able to get into and out of situations almost without detection and prove to be incredibly adept at sneaking. Finally, Enchenda citizens are selfless."

"How is that useful?" I challenge.

"Because they are always thinking about the common good. Think like a leader, Tin. How can you use that to your advantage?" he asks.

My advantage? We were talking about bringing the council around to the idea that Sarcheda is strong enough to be in charge of the council. The idea is that Sarcheda is the best realm to lead Fraun. How could a realm that puts the common good ahead of its realm be useful in that endeavor? "If I could convince a leader of Enchenda that

Sarcheda keeping their power seat is in the best interest of the common good … " I trail off as I try to figure out how to end that sentence.

"If you could convince Enchenda, they could convince the council for you," Marcus finishes.

"And if they couldn't?" I ask. "If Enchenda and Sarcheda agreed but the rest of the council wouldn't fall in line? What then?"

Marcus smirks. "You tell me. What would it be worth to you, Master Tin? What would be the cost of that old-fashioned council you mentioned not wanting to let Sarcheda take control of the council and do what needs to be done?"

There's only one answer that comes to mind. The word that the council is the most afraid of. "War?" I ask, tentatively.

Marcus freezes as though considering this. "That is a strong word."

"It's the only thing I could think of that the council would fear." I deflate a little. I can't even think of a solution that will work for this problem. Perhaps we do need Renchenda.

Marcus shakes my arm. "Hey, stop looking defeated. We are brainstorming. We should never show weakness. Always keep your head up and your shoulders back. Always be projecting the image that you are the man with the perfect solution. If you look that way they will believe it.

Image is everything."

I roll my shoulders back and take a deep breath. "Try again," Marcus commands. "Tell me again that this solution would work. Convince me."

"Should I change my answer?" I ask. "Think of something better?"

"Pick an answer and convince me with your body language that your answer is the right answer."

I hold myself to my full height, shoulders back and chest out. I raise my chin a little and let my arms drift out away from my sides. "When I am King," I say, letting my voice resonate in the small room, "I will hold the first realm seat. I will keep that seat and use it to bring strength to Sarcheda. That strength will lead to a stronger Fraun. If the council tries to remove my seat from me, they will face the consequences of war. Because Sarcheda deserves that seat. There is no reason why this seat should be taken from us. We are the best realm for the job." Marcus opens his mouth like he intends to argue with me. I wave my hand in front of his face, stopping him. "There will be no arguments. Sarcheda will be in charge of that council and they will not take the seat from me."

Marcus' smile is broad. "What a wonderful idea," he answers. "That will be the platform we build your reign on."

Chapter 9

"Enough is enough," my father yells. He steps closer to me. I am in my room, sitting cross-legged on the floor. I had been attempting to practice keeping my face calm and even. According to Marcus, when I speak with people I don't agree with or people who I feel are below me, I show it on my face. He instructed me to practice keeping my face even and calm while thinking of things that make me angry or frustrated. My father threw my door open, slamming it back against the rock wall, and yelled to make his presence known.

I blink at him, hoping it comes across as calm. "Excuse me?"

He steps closer to me but continues to use a loud voice. "You are approaching sixteen annuals. You have been an adult in all aspects of Fraun law for almost a full annual. Soon I will be able to say that ten lunar cycles have come and gone with my only son being an adult in the eyes of the kingdom and yet he has no wife. He is certainly not any closer to bringing a child into the world that has the royal blood of Sarcheda."

I take a breath, careful not to let any emotion through to my face. This is actually good practice, I realize. My father is bringing up a lot of anger right now. I can control this. It's a test. Maybe I can control this conversation as well as my face. "I'm sorry you feel that way," I begin.

I see his mouth open, but he is taking a deep breath. I have a heartbeat of time before whatever he is preparing to say comes launching out of his mouth. "I met someone." The lie is the easiest way to get his anger in check. I feel no guilt in offering him false hope. His mouth snaps closed. I have to capitalize on this upper hand. I need a believable lie. An image of the Enchenda Princess wet up to her thighs from wading through the river, pops into my head. "She's a bit younger than me," I explain, "but she is friendly and seems to understand the unique challenges that come with being Prince."

"Do I get to meet this young lady?" He doesn't ask about her blood because, to him, it doesn't matter. She could be a pauper or a highborn, a roach hand, or a teacher. She could even be Princess in another realm. Whoever she is, in the eyes of my father, she would lose all traces of her previous identity on the day she decided to marry the Prince of Sarcheda. It's that simple for him.

"Not yet," I tell him. "She's a bit shy. Give me more time to win her over."

Behind my father I see Toby standing near the

doorway. He is likely waiting to come in and clean the fireplace. I decide not to keep this conversation going longer than I can handle. "Father, if you'll excuse me, the servant has tasks to complete in here."

It's a testament to how much I've managed to take control of this conversation and calm the king that he doesn't bellow at me to stop thinking of the servants as important. Instead, he looks over his shoulder and then turns back to me. "You will let me know the moment she is ready for dinner with our family. We will show her the finest things Sarcheda has to offer."

I nod and offer a smile that looks like agreement. The king leaves the room. "Toby, you can come in now." I stand up off the floor and head for the wooden armoire that holds my clothing. "I assume you're here for the fireplace."

"Actually, I had something I needed to request."

The wooden door of the armoire is in my hand, almost closed. I push it back until it clicks shut again. "Request away," I say.

When Toby doesn't immediately begin talking, I turn around and look at him. Something about his posture is all off. He is shuffling his feet, staring at them like they're moving on their own and he's trying to figure them out. What could this boy possibly be bringing to me that has him so nervous? "Toby," I prompt.

He looks up at me and nods. "Right. My family

asked me to come and talk to you. We need a favor of sorts. I don't expect you to give me special treatment. I just don't know the proper channels for this kind of thing. If you could just point me toward who I should request this of—"

I wave my hand, effectively cutting him off. "Just tell me the request."

"Right." He takes a deep breath and stops the shuffling of his feet. Then he meets my gaze head-on. "The roof of our house was damaged in the last windstorm. We need permission to fix it."

"That's an easy one. The head of your household will come before the king during the open sessions and make the request."

"He did," Toby says. I cock one eyebrow in a silent question and wait for the servant to continue. "Your father denied the request for a new roof. He claims Sarcheda has reached its building limit for this annual. We will have to wait for three lunar cycles before we are allowed to request again."

"I'm sorry, Toby. But you requested something from the king and you received your answer. What is it, exactly, you want me to do about it?"

"We cannot afford to wait three full lunar cycles in a house with no roof, Prince Tin. Surely you see that. My family has nowhere else to stay."

I take a step closer to the boy. "You should have made this plea clearer to the king himself. Are you trying to take advantage of my kindness in giving you this position and paying your wages?"

Toby vehemently shakes his head. "No, I don't want an advantage. I was just hoping you could recommend another path, a way to try something different. Perhaps there's an empty building we could take on. Or a place you know of that we can stay. Maybe there's a loophole, like allowing neighbors to help us rebuild the roof without needing permission from the council. Surely you know of something. I see you studying policy scrolls all the time."

I force myself to look like I'm thinking. I squint my eyes a little and keep silent. He lets me think. There are ways to sidestep the rules. If they're talking about repairing a roof they don't need the permission of the king at all. The king's permission would be for an upgrade in materials or size, or for brand new. If they are simply repairing by using the same materials in the same way they were previously used, it's completely allowed. No questions asked. But Toby has put me in an interesting spot. The king has already ruled on this issue. Now, I could earn favor with a citizen and my servant if I were to simply point out this little detail. But if the king were to find out I went behind his back and gave advice on a topic he had already ruled on, he would be angry. What if there is something behind his answer that I do not know? Surely it would be better for me to wait on this until I have all the information.

"I can't think of anything right now," I say. I hold

up my finger. "But I am going to look into it a little. Perhaps I can even talk with the king myself and see what he suggests." I turn back to my armoire. "I will bring it up at dinner."

I hear the sound of scuffling behind me. "Thank you, Majesty," he says.

I get up and leave the room, deciding that two people storming into what is supposed to be a private space is not working for me. Instead, I plan to wander the grounds and get some fresh air.

Marcus is standing in the hallway when I exit my room. His arms are folded across his chest and he is leaning back against the wall. But his eyes are narrowed in my direction and he looks angry. "A word, Prince," he says.

I stop where I am in my doorway and lean on the wood. "What do you need? I was about to take a walk."

"This will not take long," he assures me. "I heard that boy ask you for a favor. I wondered if you were considering trying to help him out."

I wave my hand dismissively. "I don't know anything about that boy or his family troubles. I don't need to get involved in trivial matters. I am sure the king listened to his troubles."

"You are in a tough situation with that boy coming to you. On one hand, you should try to help him and keep up the relationship you two have cultivated. On the other hand, your father has already ruled on this particular instance. I'm sure he would have something to say about you meddling in the situation."

"As I said, I don't know anything beyond what Toby told me. I trust that the king had his reasons."

"He did," Marcus says. The way he delivers the words gives me the impression this tutor knows more than he's letting on. More than I know.

I push myself off the wood of the door jam and step toward my tutor. "Are you aware of this situation? Were you, perhaps, present when the king made his ruling?"

"I was in the room, yes."

"Give me the insight, Marcus. Why did father rule on the matter in the way that he did?"

"In my opinion, your father ruled on it out of anger. He had no reason to deny this man the right to rebuild his roof using materials he was already allotted—"

"That's exactly what I was thinking," I interrupt.

Marcus frowns at me. I close my mouth and give him a sheepish look as an apology. He clears his throat and continues. "As I was saying, I don't think there was a legal reason for the denial. In my opinion, the king saw nothing in this particular family's story that can help him in any way. In other words, he wanted a reason to grant this request. He wanted that family to do something for him."

"They are Sarcheda citizens in good standing," I say. I don't know the second part of this claim for certain, having never met them myself, but I can speculate. There is no reason why this particular family wouldn't be respected throughout the realm. They are, after all, Sarcheda.

"They are," he agrees.

"Then I don't understand. What is the problem?"

"The problem is, simply, that your father is the final voice in this realm. He enjoys exercising that right to tell people no whenever it suits him. Sometimes, I believe, he tells people no specifically to show that he is the final word."

In my own experiences with my father, this is exactly right. I didn't imagine he would be extending the same callous behavior to his citizens. "The roof can be rebuilt," I say. "It's not even something they needed to come before Father for."

"Technically, that is correct," Marcus says.

"So he told them no on an issue he didn't need to rule on as …" I pause and consider what I'm accusing my father of. "It's punishment," I decide. "Punishment for not knowing that they didn't need to ask." My blood boils with rage as I think about this. My father lives to punish. If I put a toe out of line, my father will slash with his sword to cut it off. I have to be quick enough to move it back behind the line and apologize for the way it looked to anyone watching. He is cruel for the sake of being cruel. I suddenly do not doubt that my father has been punishing the great citizens of Sarcheda in the same manner for all the time that he has been ruling. "Punishing his citizens is more important to him than keeping them happy," I say. I feel the statement as a growl in my chest.

"It appears that way," Marcus agrees. "What will you do about that?"

What will I do about that? That is the big question, isn't it? Would Sarcheda be better with me at the helm, taking these requests and doing the best I can to keep our realm the best it can be? How would I go about taking the rule from him?

But I don't have to do all that today. I need a small act capable of showing my father that I know what he's up to. One that will show the citizens I'm on their side. One that will earn me their support and favor.

"For starters," I say, "I'm going to get that roof patched."

Chapter 10

oby is easy to find. He's in the first place I look, crouched down in front of my fireplace in the bedroom, brushing ash to the front. "Toby," I call. He startles and sits back on his heels to look at me.

"Majesty?"

"You don't need permission to fix that roof," I tell him. At the surprised look on his face, I rush on. "You're not building anything new. You're patching and repairing." He looks nervous and skeptical. "I double-checked with my personal tutor. You're all set. I'm going to head into town right now and find you a few Fraunians who can help get it done. I wouldn't have told you at all, except that I realize I have no idea where your home is. Can you point it out?"

"Of course." He stands and brushes his hands down the front of his pants to knock the ashes off his fingers. "Right now?"

"Right now," I agree. In my opinion, the sooner we can get this going the sooner the community can see that I will be the kind of ruler who gets things done. The sooner they'll see that I can do for them what my father never had the guts to do. I will do what Sarcheda needs. I don't need a council to tell me what is allowed and what is not.

"I have chores and things here, Majesty. Can it wait until I am done?"

I shake my head. "No, this is more important."

"But the pay—"

I wave my hand, cutting off his objection. "You will be paid."

Toby and I have no trouble finding citizens to help us with the task. All I have to do is walk by groups of Fraunians and make a statement like "I could use your help" and people follow me. By the time we reach Toby's family home near the center of Sarcheda, we are being followed by ten large men capable of lifting much. I point to the roof. "That roof was damaged in a storm and we will need to repair it today."

I expect arguments. I brace myself for them. I expect to have to remind people that we do not need the council's permission to repair it. I expect I'll need to push out my chest and remind these men that I am their prince.

None of that is necessary.

Immediately, the men get to work. I stand back and watch, my arms crossed across my chest, as they take the broken board from the top of the house. An older man, one who looks remarkably like young Toby, comes outside. He watches for a beat before Toby goes to stand beside him.

They have a whispered conversation, the old man's eyes darting to me. I smile. Finally, he steps forward and takes charge. "We will not be improving the roof at all," he orders. "You are to help me patch the broken pieces and that is all."

The men make various noises to show their agreement. They work quickly. The boards that were splintered during the storm are taken off, there are three of them. Then one of the taller men directs them through the plan for patching the boards. They will cut off the ends, the part that used to hang below the edge of the roof. Then they will use that to patch the splintered holes in the boards.

I'm impressed, to say the least. I spend most of my days in the home of my family. Between strength training, history lessons, and studying scrolls of policy, I don't normally have much of each day remaining. How do these men even know how to do these things?

I watch as they carry out the process that was described. The boards are cut using something they call a saw. Then a few of the smaller guys climb up onto the roof of Toby's house and attach everything like a puzzle.

The man I have learned is Toby's dad stands beside the house, helping to hand everything up. He smiles in approval as the last piece is banged into place. Then he crosses the lawn and holds his hand out to me. "Thank you for arranging this entire thing, Prince Tin."

I shake his hand, feeling oddly uncomfortable at this display of camaraderie. Usually people in Sarcheda bow to me instead of shaking my hand. "No problem," I say. "It turns out you didn't need that permission after all."

"That's what Toby tried to explain," he says. "I don't think that fully makes sense to me. Why wouldn't the king tell me that himself when I asked?"

I shrug. "The king misunderstood. He thought you wanted to build brand new. The fact that you only want to repair means you have automatic permission from the council."

He nods. "I'll take your word for that. What's done is done." He turns and looks at his house. "I only hope we don't need to take it down again."

The words sting as if he had slapped me. Does he not trust me to be right? Does he not think that I have the authority to approve this? I put my hand on his shoulder and apply a little pressure. He turns his head back toward me, concern written on his face. "You had the permission of the Prince of Sarcheda to build that roof," I tell him. "No one will make you take it down. If anyone tries, you send them to me."

His resulting nod is wary and nervous. A zing of pleasure crosses my stomach. I am reminded again, at that moment, how much I love the fear of others. This is my gift, my power. This is what I bring to the kingdom: a sense of fear so great that I can use it to do what is right for the citizens of Sarcheda.

At dinner that night, with my parents, I am careful to control the pride I'm feeling. It seems like I'd be inviting confrontation to be openly bragging about what I did today. This isn't to say I'm ashamed of it, just cautious.

"What did you do all day?" Father asks.

"Nothing unusual." I try to hide my annoyance at being asked. I watch him carefully, wondering if this will be the moment when he challenges me and I have no choice but to stand up to him and be honest.

Apparently not. He resumes eating, his eyes completely focused on the food in front of him. I shrug and do the same, ignoring him completely. I'm just about done with my meal when the door to the room opens and Marcus comes in. "A word, Majesty," he says to Father. The king rises from his seat and crosses to Marcus. The two of them whisper in the doorway. Try as I may, I cannot possibly hear what they're discussing. My back is toward the two of them, meaning I cannot even see their expressions.

I lean a little back in my chair, hoping to get closer to the conversation. My mother reaches toward my hand. "Stop," she hisses. "He'll see you."

"What are they talking about?" I whisper.

She doesn't answer me right away. Instead, she settles herself back in her chair, looking like the picture of relaxation. But her head is tilted slightly to the right, her eyes are focused in the direction of the two men having a whispered conversation across the room. Then they flit back to me. "No idea," she says. "But it looks tense."

Tense could mean the king is angry when he comes back to the table. "Any idea what it could be about? Did something happen today?"

Mother shrugs, which is as I would expect. As far as I know, she doesn't leave the house during the day and doesn't seem to have anyone who comes by to speak with her about happenings in the kingdom. She wouldn't know current events if they ran her over with a roach carriage at top speed.

I sigh and take another bite of my meal, trying to ignore the curiosity burning inside me. "That's my ruling." The king's voice booms out over the room right before his stomping feet come back to the table. He drops into the chair at the head of the table and I feel his eyes burning into me.

I look up. "What was that all about?" I risk asking.

"King business," he answers. He smiles at me. "Someday you'll be allowed to have a whispered conversation with someone about a citizen in your realm who makes a terrible overstep and you can choose not to tell your obnoxious, nosy son about it."

My anger simmers under the surface, but I leave it alone. Right now, he seems positively giddy about whatever decision he just made. I equate it to how I felt this afternoon, choosing to help Toby's family rebuild their roof.

It's not my concern. A happy king does not strike his son. More importantly, a happy king does not strike his wife. I will leave this. For now.

Chapter 11

My repetitions of strength training the next morning draw a smaller crowd than usual. I run through the routine without commenting on the lack of spectators. I try not to let it draw my attention as I run through the usual warm-up, fifty push-offs, and fifty lifts of the bar. Then I hop to my feet. My trainer has surrounded the ground near him with ten of the blocks we use for competitions. He tips his head toward one. "Competition is in a fortnight," he says.

He's right. I should practice lifting. Of course, that thought brings another on its heels. There should be a larger crowd today with competition on the horizon. I take my time stacking five blocks, a warm-up, as I also scan the surrounding area for any sign that may indicate where all the citizens are today. No smoke rises from the sky, I hear no loud noises, and there are no obvious crowds on the outskirts of my vision. So where is everyone?

I lift the stack of five blocks easily, lower it until it is almost on the ground, and lift it again. I repeat this five times before setting it back on the ground. A group of young men, likely around Toby's age, clap for the display.

The thought of Toby reminds me that I haven't seen the boy yet this sun. "Have you seen my servant this morning?" I ask the trainer.

He shrugs, "Not my concern."

"How about my tutor, Marcus?"

"He was here before you were. If you had been on time you would have seen him," he scolds.

I was not that late. But I do not point this out to him because late is late. I make a mental note to not let it happen again. "Did he say if he was coming back by here later? I'd like to see if he has seen my servant."

The trainer takes a step closer to me, his large frame shaking the ground below his feet. "Do I look like I keep his schedule? Lift again."

I sigh and pick the blocks up. Again I do five repetitions of the stack before putting them down. My arms feel the strain this time. Although five blocks is nothing for me, this repetition makes it feel as though it is much heavier. If I had to do this in competition a judge would certainly see the signs of the pressure in my spasming muscles.

After I set the blocks down I pull my arm across the front of my torso and apply pressure to the elbow, stretching the muscle. I switch arms and repeat the process. My shoulder gives an audible pop.

My trainer tips his head toward the blocks I am not

using. The signal is direct and obvious. Even if I didn't feel like applying my stress and tension toward lifting today I could not ignore that signal. He wants me to add another block and repeat.

I cross the clearing and wrap my arms around a block. A defiant streak ripples through me. A violent need to refuse to do something simply because it was suggested by someone else. I try to talk myself out of it, reminding myself I was planning on lifting today anyway. But the voice refuses to be silenced.

I take the block to another that I wasn't using and drop it on top. Then I carry the two blocks across the space to the pile I had already amassed, bringing my total to seven.

"One more block was too easy for you?" my trainer asks.

I channel all my anger into giving him a defiant stare. "I need a challenge."

He shrugs as I ready myself for the lift. There are murmurs from the boys assembled beside me. I try to ignore them, rotate my neck around, and feel something give a satisfying pop. I center myself again. The murmurs resume.

I spin around. "Do you mind?" I roar. "I'm trying to focus here, I could use a little quiet."

The voices stop and the eyes of the boys turn to take in one at the back of the group that I'm certain was not there before. Toby, tear tracks running down his face, is standing behind them. He doesn't signal me or show any sign that he was here looking for me.

I decide to pretend not to see him. We are not friends, I remind myself. I put my focus on the seven blocks. Again, they lift easily. Again, I lower them almost to the ground and then rise again. This time I only get four repetitions in before I can feel the tremble in my legs. I force the fifth lift anyway before setting the blocks down.

Then I turn to my trainer. "I'm running," I tell him. My voice is stern, challenging. He merely nods in response. I look at the group, careful to keep my eyes away from Toby's. "If my servant has something to say he will have to keep up." I break into a jog and move out away from the village and toward the ravine.

Three houses away from the clearing I slow down just a little. I want to give the appearance that I am still going as quickly as I can, but I cannot hear whether or not there are footsteps behind me. My curiosity is piqued and I want to know if Toby has come along for the run.

Two houses further I have determined I am hearing footsteps and they are not moving as quickly as I am. There are fewer citizens out this far, as well. Even if I were to pass someone, they would not be aware of the pace I was jogging when I started my run today. I slow down again.

I count to fifteen before Toby's footsteps sound like they are catching up. "Apparently you did need something,"

I say.

Toby's voice gives away his struggle to breathe. "I just need ..."

I stop and turn to face him. His face is red, his breathing coming fast. He doubles over, resting his hands on his knees. Clearly whatever he has to say is going to wait. I see a nearby water trough and make my way over to it. Toby doesn't follow. I dip my hands into the lukewarm water and splash it on my face and chest. Then I cup my hands and fill them. I lean down and drink. The water isn't as fresh as I've had before, but it satisfies my thirst. By the time I have taken my second cupping of water, Toby has joined me. He helps himself to a drink then turns to face me.

"Let's hear what you have to say," I prompt.

"My father is dead," he says.

I'm surprised at the strength of his voice and the intensity of his gaze. I blink a few times, trying to find words. "I'm sorry," I say. "When did that happen?" I just saw his father yesterday. We just rebuilt the roof. I have a heartbeat of fear wondering if the roof may have collapsed in the night. But if that were the case those men I hired would be at fault. Surely I could find them again, bring justice.

"Last night. He was killed." Toby takes a step toward me in a show of strength I didn't know he was capable of before today. "Your father killed him."

I blink a few times, trying to process all the information. "That is a big accusation."

"It's not an accusation. A man showed up at our door last night. He asked for my father by name. He stood him on our front lawn and read a scroll from the king. My father was tried for crimes against the king, acting on an issue that has previously been banned by the king. He was beheaded for his crime."

The thoughts in my head come quickly. At first, I think he's lying, but I dismiss that because of the pain clearly visible on his face. Then I think someone has set my father up, but just as quickly the truth rushes in like storm clouds. The dinner. Marcus disrupted our dinner to speak with my father about something. My father's parting words echo in my head: "That's my ruling".

I run my hands down my face as if I can wipe away this mistake. My father has always been cruel to me, that is not new. But this is a new level. That roof was completely rebuilt using materials that were already appropriated for the roof. They didn't even need permission. He is angry at me for showing them this. He is angry at me because he thinks I disobeyed him. This is a punishment for me.

I reach toward Toby and he takes a step back. It is that act that reminds me we are not friends. Perhaps that is what my father set out to prove. He thinks I have become soft with this servant. He thinks I am weak. He has set a trap here to prove it. I already helped this boy once, if I help him again my father will see me for what I am.

I pull my hand back, tying it up with my other hand behind my back. "I am sorry to hear that."

"Will you speak with your father?" he asks.

"What would be the point in that? Would my confrontation bring your father back?"

Toby shakes his head. "You said we didn't need permission. We didn't know you went behind his back."

"What's done is done," I say. "You have the roof you needed. You have the roof that was so important. Your family will make it through the next few lunar cycles without having to move to a new residence. There's nothing we can do to change it." I keep my voice level, even, and unemotional. This is not the outcome I wanted when I helped him. I can see his pain plainly on his face and I feel it tugging at my heart but I cannot relent. I cannot connect with him. I cannot share this. I cannot be weak.

My father is coming for me, I can feel it. It would be better for everyone if no one is blocking his path to me when he comes.

"You are a monster," Toby says. His voice is low as if this is a secret he has just learned.

"I am a prince of strength," I correct. "We made a decision and carried it out." I turn my back on Toby. "I am going to finish my run if there is nothing more you need to say to me." I count two full breath cycles without a word from Toby before I start jogging.

I am only one house away when I hear him break down into tears behind me. I increase my speed until it physically hurts. Then I increase the speed again. This is the pain I deserve. I am a monster.

Chapter 12

The next morning there is a loud bang as the door to my chambers is thrown open. I jump in surprise and then, when I see who is standing in the doorway, immediately hate myself for doing that. My father surely saw that twitch and saw it as a sign of weakness.

I take notice of how much sunlight is coming into the room. We are supposed to be traveling to Renchenda today to pick up some crops and a new roach. Apparently, the entire family making the travel is going to send the right message to Renchenda. Show them we are a cohesive family or some such nonsense. Judging by the sun, I am not late for our departure. I take my time standing up. "Are you ready?" Father asks. "Or are we waiting for you to put on a clean dress or something?"

"Was that supposed to be an insult?" I challenge. I'm still seething about the news yesterday. This man thought it would be appropriate to challenge me by killing someone from Sarcheda. How are we supposed to earn the respect of Sarcheda citizens if we think they are expendable? They should be the least expendable citizens in the kingdom. We should be doing everything in our power to protect them.

He narrows his eyes at me. "It's only an insult if you think it was."

I do not take the bait. Instead, I take a glance down at the clothes I am wearing and decide they will be fine for a journey like the one we are undertaking. I physically push my father aside and walk out of the doorway. I'm aware that he must have let me push him, he's stronger than I am and we both know it. But I keep walking with my head held high until I am out the front door and facing a small carriage.

Mother is already standing there. So is my father's servant. But the shocking part is Toby, sitting on top of the small carriage with the reins for the two roaches in his hands. "What is he doing here?" I ask, pointing to the younger Fraunian.

"We travel with our servants because we can afford to. That is the message we are sending. Get in the carriage," Father answers.

The carriage looks small. It looks like the three of us will be crammed if we all get inside. But this is not the battle I want to wage today. I have more important ones to fight. I climb inside the carriage and sit nearest the door. My mother climbs in and shuffles past me to sit beside me, closest to the only window in the carriage. She folds her hands into her lap and looks down at the floor. When the king climbs in the carriage rocks as if he is determined to make as much of an entrance as possible even in this small space. He drops into the bench opposite us. "Go," he bellows.

When the carriage doesn't immediately begin moving, he bangs on the wall behind him. "Go," he hollers again.

I roll my eyes. His servant would have to climb up on the bench beside Toby. Likely the older man is the one who will be driving, meaning he has to take the reins from Toby. There is no reason to assume this will all happen as quickly as my father can drop his rear into a bench inside a carriage that is too small for three people. Again, I stop myself from starting this fight. This is not the fight I want today either. I must be careful when I pick my moment because it is likely I will only get one.

We travel in silence down the center of town toward Renchenda. Part of me hopes it will stay this silent all the way there. But I know better. I know it won't be long before the king says or does something to instigate me. He will see it as fun, especially because I know my body language gives away how tense I am right now. I am angry with the king. I am disappointed in the man I thought he could be. More importantly, I am confident I could do a better job leading Sarcheda than he is doing. I am sure every single one of my opinions is written in my tense muscles, my crossed arms, and my scowl.

Father sighs and locks eyes with me across the carriage. He probably expects me to look away. I don't. Instead, I force my teeth together and narrow my eyes to match his. Without looking away, proving to me this is a contest of wills, he speaks. "How is your wrist feeling this morning, Alexa?" he asks.

"Fine," my mother answers. Her voice is soft and it catches on her emotion. I can't help it, I break eye contact with my father to look at my mother. She is fighting back tears, I can tell by the way her jaw is quivering. I glance down at her lap where her hands are still clasped. There is an angry purple line ringing her right wrist like a bracelet. I reach down and pull back the long sleeve of her dress, revealing three similar lines up her arm. She winces at my touch and gently tugs her arm free. Instinctively I know what those marks mean. Those are as good as fingerprints and I know exactly who left them on my mother.

I return my gaze to the king, feeling the fire burn hot inside me. I decide in the time it takes my heart to beat only twice. This is the fight we will have today. "What did you do?" My voice is low and dark like the growl of a dangerous animal.

My father actually shrugs and then a smile creeps along his cheeks. "Nothing she didn't deserve," he answers.

"Stop the carriage," I yell. I do not wait for it to come to a complete stop before flinging open the only door. I jump out, my anger propelling me forward. I land awkwardly in the dirt, stumbling.

My father climbs slowly out of the carriage. He is in full control of his body, like always. He stands to his full height, one mark over my head, and looks down his nose at me. "You are so weak, it's pathetic." His voice is a low rumble, echoing over the ravine behind me.

At my side, my hands curl into fists automatically. I grind my teeth. I'm so tired of his taunting. I'm tired of never being good enough for him. I'm tired of him always looking for the weakest person to take out his anger on. I'm tired of him torturing my mother and innocent Sarcheda citizens just to get a reaction out of me. I'm tired of being the person he thinks is too weak. I'm tired of trying to prove myself to a father that will never think I'm good enough.

He steps back. For one heartbeat I think I've won. Then I see his eyes fall on my clenched fists. When his eyes return to my face, he smiles. "You don't have the guts to use those." He leans toward me. "I dare you to hit me. I'll give you one free shot. But if there are two shots I should warn you I'll hit back."

Mom steps out of the carriage, her hands up. "Alright, alright. Enough." She steps toward us, pushing her hands out between us. I feel her palm on the center of my chest, pushing back. Her touch is light, reminding me of the reason we're standing here. The anger hums again. "There are people watching." Her eyes dart back to the carriage. "This is not befitting of royalty."

She's right. Of course, she's right. I let my shoulders drop down a notch and transfer my weight to my back foot. "Besides," she continues, "you aren't stupid enough to take on the King of Strength, Tin."

A chuckle slips out of the king's lips. "Good thing your Mom was here to save you," he says.

With just that comment, the anger returns. I raise my arm, knocking the queen away from me. I drop my hand on her shoulder, hard, and squeeze a little. I am warning her to back off with just that simple gesture. Her eyes widen and her breathing quickens. I feel a rush of power. I let that power wash over me before I look back to my father. I hope he can see the power in my face.

"I could do it, you know," I say. I don't know why I say it. I don't even know what I was threatening. But once it's out there, the idea starts to gain momentum. I turn my head, looking around. "I could throw her down that ravine right there." I turn back to my father. "Then you'd travel into Renchenda and have to explain that image." I take a step toward him. "I'd shut her up good. She'd never have an opinion again." I notice, over the king's shoulder, Toby and my father's servant are both watching. Good. "I'd be better at shutting her up than you ever were." I take another step, close enough now that I could strike him if I wanted to. "I'll be a better ruler than you ever were either. I don't need my mother for that."

"You don't have the balls," the King says. He's talking through clenched teeth. He's angry. If I give him the chance, he'll knock me down hard. I roll my shoulders back just a little. I'm not backing down. Not this time. "You've always been too weak to be my heir," he says. "I will never give you my throne and you don't have the strength you would need to take it away from me."

I feel my anger build beyond what I ever thought possible. Annuals of him talking down to me like this boil in my blood. I look at my mother, maybe I'm looking for something that will talk me out of it. But she's looking at him. She's looking at him like she still sees something good inside him, like she may still love him. She's completely blind. She's always been blind. She ignores how he treats me. She ignores the bad things he's done. In the end, I don't apologize. I clamp one hand on her shoulder and the other on her hip. I spin her body like it weighs nothing. I push her to the edge.

I could stop. I should stop.

But she stumbles, catches herself, and smiles. It's almost like some part of her is proud of me for doing what he wanted. Almost like she agrees with his parenting style. The rage boils again.

"He's going to be so proud of you," she whispers.

Suddenly, I don't want to make him proud. I want this to be over, once and for all.

I rush at her, knocking her over the edge.

I see her fall and my heart misses a beat. What have I done?

Behind me, the King begins clapping. Slowly at first, but then with increased speed. "Who knew you had it in you, kid?"

I turn and face him. I expect sadness of the magnitude I'm suddenly feeling to be mirrored on his face. I expect pain and shock. Instead, I see a smile. He steps closer to me. "I must say, I didn't expect that." He stops and jabs a finger into my chest. "But it's not the throne. Not yet."

He's right. It's not. It wasn't her fault he's been this way my entire life. It's his. I put my right foot closer to him and lean on it, drawing myself closer to his frame.

He shakes his head. "You think you can take me out, boy?" He leans in until our noses practically touch. "You want to know a secret, son? I'd feel nothing but pride if you had what it takes to seize this throne right here and right now. It would be the ultimate show of strength. It would show these people right here that you are the rightful King of Sarcheda." He straightens up and uses that obnoxious voice he reserves for crowds. "Go ahead and show them. Show these two servants that you have what it takes to make decisions for Sarcheda even when they're not the easy decisions."

"Like killing a citizen for doing something allowed by the council?" I challenge. "Like bruising your own wive's wrist? Or maybe you mean the hard things like smacking around your only son?"

"Or like pushing your mother off a ravine," he says.

That deflates me a little. Suddenly, I want to run to the ravine and look for my mother. I want to offer her my hand and pull her back up. This was a mistake. The whole argument was a mistake. I've let my father turn me into a monster.

I take a step back from him.

The sound of his laughter rings through the area, bouncing off the carriage so that it feels like I'm being enveloped by it. "I knew it," he says. "I knew you were weak. You don't even have the guts to take out someone you hate."

I don't argue. How can I? He's right. I hang my head as he takes a step away from me and turns to face the servants. I will never have what it takes to lead Sarcheda.

"The day this kid does anything that makes me proud, I'll die of shock," my father says. The old servant laughs.

But Toby doesn't. Toby is looking past my father, right at me. He's looking at me with a fear I have never seen before. As if I am unpredictable. As if I am dangerous.

I am dangerous. I am unpredictable.

But in this case, I also know I'm right. I am better than the king.

If the two of us are pitted against each other, I am the lesser of the two monsters.

I set my jaw and run at my father.

I catch him off guard, which is probably the only reason why it works. My shoulder hits him square in his chest and I watch as he topples toward the ravine. I fall with him, my momentum carrying me. For a beat, I think this is it. The ultimate ending. We are both about to fall to our deaths.

But I catch myself on the edge, pull myself back up and flop on my stomach. Then I look down. From this perch atop the ravine, I watch my father fall.

He never yells.

For the first time in my life, he doesn't even look angry.

I lay there, on my stomach, until I can no longer see him. Then I stand up and face the two servants who are watching me with horror on their faces. "There was an accident here," I say. I swallow the last of my doubts, they're small enough to go down without a fight. I will take control of this situation. I will take control of Sarcheda. "The king and queen fell from the overturned cart to their deaths. I was lucky to escape with my life."

I stare pointedly at the two men. "You heard the exchange. You know what kind of man he was. The question now is this: did either of you survive the accident? Because if you aren't sure what story you will tell when we arrive back in Sarcheda, your tragic death will be another that happens right here on the edge of the greatest realm in the kingdom."

Father's servant bows before me. "It was the ant that ran in front of us that did it, Majesty. I swerved to avoid it and tipped the cart. My apologies."

"That is what happened and you are pardoned by your new king," I tell him. "You are my servant now, what is your name?"

"Call me Ben, Majesty. I live to serve you."

I turn my eyes to Toby. "Did you survive the accident?" I ask.

He looks one loud noise away from tears. "You just killed your parents," he whispers.

I cross the space between us in three large steps until I am nose to nose with the boy who has served me for more than an annual "Say that again and you will join them. It was an accident. Choose which story you are planning on repeating." I pause for a heartbeat. "Say it," I yell.

Toby flinches. "It was an accident," he repeats.

"Do I need to worry about you?" I ask.

"No. Of course not. No." He shakes his head violently.

"Good," I tell him. I straighten back up. "You don't want a king for an enemy," I say.

Chapter 13

By the morning I am sworn in as King a few things have changed. The most obvious is that people in Sarcheda have doubts about the king and queen having an accident that would have caused their deaths. Fraunians doubt my story. But it doesn't threaten my rule. Instead, it has made them all afraid of me. As I have long suspected, the power of fear is strong. It is just one more way I will be the best ruler Sarcheda has ever had.

The second thing that has changed is my servant. He has gone missing from Sarcheda. Part of me is concerned, will he tell what he saw? But mostly, if I'm being honest, I miss having him around. He was someone I could count on to be on my side at all times. Without him here, I have to trust Marcus.

Marcus is the third change. Sure, he knows I am King and accepts me as King. But, in private, he still tries to control me like he used to. I'm dealing with it, but I feel like I have to be on my toes around him.

There's a knock at the door, light and delicate.

"Come in," I yell. I'm in Castle Fraun, in a small room on the first floor. Renchenda houses all of our formal events inside the Castle. Babies born, new kings, and wedding announcements are all held here. I hate that I have to be announced as King of Sarcheda from Renchenda. That is one thing that I will try to change on my council.

The wooden door opens and a person with impressive height but a young face enters. "You are the new king?" he asks. He has blond hair that is covering his forehead. I don't recognize him. His clothes are tailored, meaning he is more likely to be royalty than he is to be a commoner working in the castle. He is wearing orange, which is the color of Renchenda. This could be an accident, especially if he was a common citizen. But tailored orange clothing on the day of a formal event means he is likely royalty of Renchenda. There is only one royal in Renchenda who is young enough to be this boy.

I hold my hand out to him. "I am King Tin. I assume you are Prince Jordyn?"

He shakes my hand, his grip is weaker than I would expect from a boy his age. I try not to scowl at him, reminding myself that strength is not valued in his realm. "You look young for leading a realm," he notes. "How do you feel about ruling? Are you scared of what will happen in council? What happened to your parents?" he asks all these questions in quick succession.

I cock my eyebrow, trying to decide if this boy is

insulting me with his insinuations. "That is a lot of questions," I say. "I feel like I am capable of ruling. Like you, I spent my childhood training for this. I'm not scared of anything, especially that old-fashioned council. As for my parents, they had an accident."

"What kind of accident?" he presses.

"Why do you ask?"

He frowns. "Sorry, am I being rude? I am curious. I like to know things so I ask a lot of questions. My father says I need to learn to control it before I am a king."

That's true, this boy will one day be King. I smile at him. "Curiosity is healthy. My parents' carriage was overturned near the ravine. They fell to their deaths."

"Were you in the carriage?" he asks, tilting his head to the side as if trying to gauge my reaction.

I make my face look properly sad. "I was. Luckily, I was spared. Honestly, my head went past the edge and I thought, for a heartbeat, that it was over for me as well." Sprinkling in this piece of honesty allows me to look emotional. "I had to watch my father fall. It was a moment that will forever be etched on my memory."

Prince Jordyn allows a respectful silence. Then he squints his eyes at me. "How old are you?"

"Sixteen annuals."

"I was right, you are young to be a king."

I straighten myself to full height and puff out my chest. This boy has quite a few clicks on me, which is frustrating. But I am King and he is merely a prince. "I will be the king Sarcheda needs, regardless of my age."

He offers me his hand. "Good luck, King Tin."

I accept the handshake. The boy turns to leave the room. When his hand is on the door, I call out to him. "How old are you?"

He answers without turning around. "Fourteen annuals."

So this is to be his full height. Good. He is already the tallest citizen I have met. "Have your parents greyed?" I ask. I would like to know how long I have to try and influence this boy before he is sitting at the council table with me.

"No." The answer is simple but something about it rings with a sadness I didn't expect. I wonder if it is the thought of his parents that makes him sad or the thought of them dying. I don't fully understand either emotion, honestly. There is not a part of me that regrets what happened to my parents. My father was a terrible king and my mother was weak.

Sarcheda, and Fraun, will be stronger with me at the helm. Under my direction, Fraun will be forever changed.

About the Author

Tabatha Shipley is an author, avid reader, and book addict from Arizona. She has an amazing husband, two remarkable children, and one really quirky dog. She can often be found on social media raving about whatever book she is most recently obsessed with. Find her to join in on the obsession and add to her TBR with your favorite titles.

tabathashipleybooks.com

www.ingramcontent.com/pod-product-compliance
Lightning Source LLC
Chambersburg PA
CBHW061206210726
48294CB00006B/1771